THE *Green* ROSE

A NOVEL BY

CLARKE LOWE
AND EUGENE L. WEEMS

THE GREEN ROSE

Copyright © 2015 by CLARKE LOWE & EUGENE L. WEEMS

This novel is a work of fiction. Any reference to real people, events, establishments, organizations or locales are intended only to give the fiction a sense of reality and authenticity. All of the main characters, organizations, events and incidents in this novel are creations of the authors' imaginations and their resemblance, if any, to actual events or persons, living or dead, is entirely coincidental.

Published by: Celebrity Spotlight Entertainment, LLC
www.celebrityspotlightentertainmentllc.com
FIRST EDITION: 2015

Cover Design: Marion Designs/www.mariondesigns.com
Editor: Terri Harper/Terristranscripts@gmail.com
ISBN: 978-1503357044
ISBN 10: 1503355704

Library of Congress Cataloguing-in-Publication Data:

Celebrity Spotlight Entertainment, LLC

Printed in the United States of America

ACKNOWLEDGMENTS

ALDINE WEEMS...My grandmother and mother, the woman who holds both titles, my world, my heart. The loving and caring spirit that intoxicates my soul. The foundation of my temple. The queen who remains at the top of the pedestal of my realm. The woman who raised such a handsome, respectful, successful man. How can I ever show or express my gratitude for being blessed with you? Such words of appreciation don't exist in this world. Memories of you, your unconditional love, kindness, and beauty remain alive through me. I will continue on my journey toward achieving all your unfinished goals as well as my own aspirations until I conquer them all. As you used to say, a person will never accomplish nothing with hopes and wishes, but only through believing in self, hard work, dedication and devotion to the things you want to see happen. My success is living proof of your teachings. Love you, momma, with all my heart and beyond my last breath.

My love goes out to the following people: My sister Melissa Gina Johnson, my niece Micaiah and nephew Micah.

Finally, my deepest appreciation and warmest friendship is extended to all those people who have been supportive. Thank you for the love. I will keep bringing you hot page turning novels. So if you missed out on any, go cop them and experience the excitement of an electrified heart throbbing read. Let me continue to take you into worlds beyond your imagination.

Eugene L. Weems

ACKNOWLEDGMENTS

Thanks to Eugene L. Weems.

It's an honor to be a part of this project.

I would also like to thank my mother Nancy Hamm
for always being there.

Clarke Lowe

TABLE OF CONTENTS

Chapter 1

Los Angeles, California

The mid afternoon was gorgeous with thin motionless clouds bordering the horizon. The rays of the sun were moderate, not as warm as one would expect for Southern California in July. Summer had been late coming this year, and it was obvious that it wasn't here with a vengeance. July had no record temperatures so far and today looked like no exception. It felt like spring.

Curtis exited the Chase Bank slightly distracted while texting on his cell phone. Dressed in his usual hip-hop attire and draped in the stereotypical hip hop artist bling jewelry, with more diamonds than one man should ever own, he blindly strolled toward his car as if he were sleep walking with his phone in his hand. Suddenly, he was startled by a loud ear piercing scream.

When Curtis looked up, he noticed a woman attempting to fend off what appeared to be some kind of sexual assault in progress. He would find out later this was not the case, but a reason for him to spring into action just the same. Without much thought, he leapt at the man who was tugging at this middle aged white woman's jacket. It looked as if the attacker was pulling at something within her inner pocket.

Curtis tackled the man as spectators along Wilshire Boulevard gawked, gasped, and began to call the authorities to report the disturbance. The assailant was no match for Curtis's street raised combat experience.

The Caucasian man was, in Curtis's opinion, in his early forties, a bit disheveled, and smelled as though he was losing in his efforts to navigate the financial struggles that come along with being a ghetto dweller from the streets.

The assailant began to concede his attempt to rob the woman and concentrate on trying to escape the grasp of a much more aggressive and experienced Curtis. The weaker man found himself struggling to breathe in the tight headlock Curtis placed him in. One of the bank employees had come out of the bank in the midst of the ruckus, apparently notified by the attack victim, and mentioned something to the tune of "Thank You" and "The police are on the way." Most of the events began to blur for Curtis, who was filled with adrenaline from the confrontation. He hardly heard anything that was said.

Before Curtis realized what he was doing, he had already begun to drag the man to his car parked fifteen feet from the bank, and began yelling to nervous spectators to grab his car keys from his pocket.

Through the crowd came a huge redneck who looked as if he were a professional body builder, and he went right for Curtis's jacket pocket. Curtis wondered where this herculean gentleman was five minutes ago. The incredible hulking spectator fumbled with the keys while Curtis continued to shout "Pop the Trunk, Pop the Trunk!"

Other spectators were saying "The cops are on the way."

Curtis responded shouting "Who's gonna hold him until they get here?" There were more than a dozen bystanders, but no one had an answer. "That's what I thought," Curtis added.

As soon as the trunk flew open, Curtis lifted his struggling captive into the air by the seat of his dirty jeans, shoved him into the trunk and slammed the lid. No sooner than the trunk closed, the police arrived.

As the uniformed police officers exited their cars, the crowd of spectators began to fill them in, all trying to speak at the same time about what they had witnessed.

Apparently, none of the statements were accurate, because at the mention of the black man putting someone in the trunk, guns were drawn and Curtis found himself in handcuffs, trying to explain to officers who didn't want to hear anything he had to say.

After almost five long minutes as a kidnapping suspect, he was suddenly being hailed as a hero. The truth is, Curtis only wanted to leave. He wasn't impressed by any of this; he just wanted to head back to his city, Oakland, where drug dealing, prostitution and murder was the normal, daily practice for many. For now though, police procedure would trump everything. Curtis stayed to give his statement, replete with residential and identification information.

Though it's been almost two weeks since the attempted robbery, not a day has passed that I haven't thought about my unpolished hero. I decided to meet with my two closest friends, Amanda and Kathryn, to help me process what had happened and finally put the incident behind me. Just before leaving, I took a brisk walk down my quarter mile long driveway to check the mail. As I walked the pathway to my mailbox, I thought how nice my home is, but despaired because my husband was never here to share it with me. After retrieving my mail and leafing through it along my walk back to my Beverly Hills mansion, I froze in my steps. I was surprised to see an envelope addressed to me from the South Hollywood Police Department.

Uncertain of what I might find inside the envelope, a flood of emotions, mainly the fear of finding a subpoena to appear in court and having to face my attacker, began to stir some anxiety. I slowly unfolded the paperwork inside. Oddly enough, I was relieved to see that it was only a copy of the completed police report and statements of the witnesses to the incident.

Being reminded of the incident that has kept me paralyzed for almost two weeks, I found myself consumed once again with fear of leaving my eight-bedroom, five-and-a-half-bath Beverly Hills fortress. Not feeling one hundred percent safe, I kept my in-house cleaning staff near, since my husband Richard was away on business, again.

Not that I would feel extremely safe with Dick, as my arrogant husband prefers to be called, for reasons I will never understand. I always expressed how I felt the name Dick is so inappropriate. His birth name is Richard Parvis Stintpindal. Where does he get Dick from? The thought eased my stress level as I smirked and continued my trek home.

Once inside, I began to relive the incident as I read through the many statements the authorities had accumulated. So many mixed feelings began to flood my thoughts, I muttered aloud *"I had no idea so many people were standing around. No one helped the roguish looking gentleman who saved my life."* Just as the thought entered my mind, I began hurriedly flipping through the documents looking for the statement of the man who had thwarted this vicious attack against me.

"Viola!" the sound escaped me before I realized my own excitement at finding his statement.

There was only one thing I was looking for, his name. Who was he? I remembered not having the opportunity to thank him or even speak to him once the police arrived. I was held up to give my report, and then observed by paramedics before being allowed to leave. During my uneventful experience with police and medical staff, the mystery man who had saved me had already been cleared and released by police.

Just as sudden as he had come into my life, he was

gone without notice. *Thank goodness for the police report*, I thought, *now I have a name. That name is Curtis, Curtis Blaine Rainier. Doesn't sound like the name of a hero and surely isn't a strong name like Richard Parvis Stintpindal,* I joked to myself and smiled. I quietly whispered, "Curtis Blaine Rainier," and smiled again as I leaned back on my sofa to raise and tuck my feet beneath me and read his statement.

While I read the statement Curtis had given, that very familiar sense of safety and security enveloped and confused me at the same time. The type of man my hero happens to be is the very type of man I had hoped to never encounter. To me, Curtis's image exemplified the stereotypical definition of a troublesome hoodlum. His thuggish attire personified that of a gang member or rap artist. Either way, I thought to myself that I more expected to be robbed by a man like Curtis before I would be robbed by a middle aged white man who looked like a gentleman down on his luck.

An odd sense of guilt caused me to feel somewhat embarrassed. I started looking through the documents once more. This time I was searching for a clue that would lead to a plan of action that I knew was long overdue.

There it was, just beneath the soft and un-heroic name, Curtis Blaine Rainier, a phone number and several addresses listed my protector's contact info: (510) 555-1282.

It was decided. "*I will call to thank him,*" I declared to myself. I, being ever so indecisive most of my life, like every other Libra according to my horoscope, called my good friend and therapist, Kathryn Fulgham.

"Kathryn Fulgham," a woman's voice came through the iPhone.

"Hi Kat, it's me, MaryAnn. I'm sorry to bother you dear, are you extremely busy?" I questioned.

"Well, hon, I have a client to see in five minutes, so I have two for you, are you okay?" Kathryn asked.

"Oh, yes, of course, I'm fine. I have a question Kat. I was thinking about calling the young man who helped me during the incident, you know, and I wanted to know what you thought about it."

"Yeah," Kathryn says, then pauses before continuing, "I think that's a great idea, MaryAnn. It's definitely progress in the right direction for putting this behind you. I absolutely have no objections. After all, it's just one call to express your gratitude, right?" Kat responded.

"Yes," I said cautiously. Then I followed with, "But what if he's not nice? He did put the robber guy in the trunk, remember? Oh my, what if he wants..."

"Calm yourself, MaryAnn, it'll be fine. I'm sure he doesn't want money and he can't be that bad of a guy. He did save your life, right?" Kathryn said reassuringly. "It's just a call, say thank you, clear your conscious and call me tomorrow, okay? I'm sorry, hon, but I have to go, my client is here. Call me tomorrow, Ta-Ta," Kathryn ended her call.

I now had the reassurance I needed. "Well, here goes." As I dialed the number, with every button I pushed my heart rate increased. The phone was ringing. One ring, two ring, three, *Oh god, please don't answer*, I silently prayed, hoping to just leave a voicemail message and be done with this mystery thug. Four rings...

"Yeah, yeah, holla at ya boy."

I froze, afraid to speak, unable to find my voice. Who answers the phone like this? I was close to hanging up.

"Say something! Who dis?" The voice said again.

"Uh, hi," I stuttered. "I'm...my name is MaryAnn, uh..."

"Spit it out lady, who are you looking for?" Said the

rude voice.

More nervous than before, words rushed out of my mouth. "My name is MaryAnn Stintpindal; I'm looking to speak with a Curtis Rainier."

"What for, and how do you know him?"

"Oh, I'm sorry, he saved my life and I just..."

"Oh yeah, you the lady that dummy tried to rape by the bank that day, huh?" The voice interrupted, still yet to acknowledge if he was in fact Curtis Rainier or not.

"Oh no," I said, "I'm afraid you're confusing me with someone else." I pondered what the man said and wondered how many women had this man saved. He must really be a hero. I continued, "No, I was in Hollywood leaving the bank and a man attempted to snatch a bank envelope from my inside coat pocket, and..."

"Oh, okay," the man interrupted again, "Snap! I thought that fool was grabbing your boobs or some shit. Yeah, I'm Curtis, little momma, are you okay?" Curtis asked in a rough sense of concern.

Oddly enough, I appreciated his concern, even though his expression and intonation was a bit aggressive and not very well articulated, I could sense his concern was genuinely sincere. "Yes, I'm fine thank you," I responded. I continued to speak, "Sir, I only wanted to thank you so very much, but you had left before I could, and I received a copy of the police report today that included your information. I hope you don't mind my calling?"

"Naw, Naw, you alright. Ain't no big deal, ma'am. I couldn't watch no woman be handled by no man in any way that could hurt or have her sad. I got a momma and I would want the same help for my moms if she was in trouble, feel me?" The man replied. I assumed I should respond with a yes, and so I did.

Though I felt as if this man appeared to be boxing

with the English language, I began to feel a strange connection and sense of security just from hearing his voice. He had a strong confident, raspy, but too deep a voice, the type of voice that would probably be better suited for a blues singer who enjoys a smooth cognac and sweet cigar every so often. He had a relaxing, disarming, and charming voice all the same.

Just when I decided to bring the conversation to an end, the man asked, "Listen Ma," short for Little momma I supposed, "I ain't busy today at all and I'll be leaving town in the morning, but I'm hungry now, so if you want to talk about it, lunch is on me if you're interested?"

Now this truly caught me off guard. It was just supposed to be a call to express my gratitude, a call to say thank you, clear your conscience and put this behind you, I remembered Kathryn, my therapist's, advice. But without warning my lips blurted "Sure, that would be nice." *Oh my god, what am I doing?* I cursed myself for having no control over my own mind. *The indecisive Libra in me is going to mean my end one day, I just know it,* I thought to myself, my mind raced a mile a minute.

"Cool." His response snapped me back to reality. "Where you want to eat at, my treat?" he said. I began to feel I had already said too much, and knew I would only feel comfortable in a crowded place in the open, but not a familiar place where I could be seen with a strange black man accompanying me.

I hesitated a moment before replying, "Rousseau's Delicatessen is a quiet place we can go, right there on Sunset, do you know it?" I asked.

"Naw, not really, I'm from the Bay Area. I'm here on business but I can Google and Mapquest it. See you there in an hour?" he asked.

"That'll be fine," I respond.

"Alright, Down," Curtis said before hanging up.

"Down? I don't understand," I declared, "Hello...Hello..." Finally I realized the man had disconnected the call. Confused and feeling a bit nostalgic, I hurried to prepare to meet Curtis. Why, I still had yet to discover. One thing is for certain though, I won't be alone, but he'll never know it. I had one more call to make before I could leave.

"Hello, Kathryn, I need you to come to Rousseau's, but I want you to wait for me across the street at the coffee house while I meet with Curtis."

"Curtis?" Kathryn inquired

"The guy who saved me the other day, remember, you said I should call and thank him."

"Oh yeah, how did that go?"

"Well, I'm meeting with him for lunch at Rousseau's, so... that's how it went."

"Rousseau's, huh? It must have gone pretty good," Kathryn said, surprised at the idea I was taking a new guy to our favorite place.

"Well, I guess so, but I'm a little worried, I'm kinda' on the fence about it. I feel really safe going out with him. I mean, he saved me, right, but I don't know him. I was hoping I could get you to be there for me, you know, like keep an eye on things for me. Maybe you could call Amanda and have her come with you. You guys could go out for coffee across the street from Rousseau's, I would feel a lot better knowing you're right over there, you know what I mean?"

"Of course MaryAnn," Kathryn reassured me, "Amanda just called me so I think it will work out perfect, we'll be there, I promise, but I'm sure you'll be fine anyway."

"Okay, thanks Kat, I knew I could count on you."

Chapter 2

Rousseau's Delicatessen was designed with an ambience that was apropos for the surrounding elite Beverly Hills neighborhood. The fine luncheon eatery had an Etruscan decor replete with marble flooring, stone Romanesque statues, ornate latticework, lush hanging vines and a warm, romantic atmosphere. Every lucky woman who walked through the door was presented with a fresh, long-stemmed rose.

I noticed him immediately when he entered the establishment. Curtis was well dressed in a neatly pressed white dress shirt open at the collar, tailored beige pants and expensive Italian dress shoes. He had a cool relaxed look as he stopped to eye the waiters skillfully tossing salads tableside. I was surprised at his change of attire. Today he had a more conservative style, but the truth is Curtis was a stranger and may be the type that you hear about on the news daily.

I had secured a table in plain sight just in case some assistance was needed from the public. I was determined to be safe, rather than sorry. I stood and got his attention, politely waving him over.

He was a complete gentleman and thoughtful in pulling out my seat. Not quite what I expected. He took a seat across the table and placed the fine cloth napkin neatly on his lap, took up a menu and shot a handsome smile my way before quickly scanning the items on the menu. He broke the silence.

"Very nice place, a bit over the top for lunch, but I guess this is how these rich white folks do it out this way. I like they style though. Since I don't see any hamburgers and fries on the menu, I'll take the rosemary chicken with mushroom ravioli, how about you?" Curtis asked.

"Oh my, the Caesar salad and side order of the crab stuffed shrimp is my favorite," I admitted

"Do you eat here often?" he asked.

"Not as often as I used to when I was a teen," I replied."I absolutely love the grilled vegetables and duck rubbed with anise and flamed in Grand Marnier, you must try it one day."

"I'll keep it in mind."

Several hours had quickly passed and Curtis and I found ourselves in conversation over ice cream sundaes like high school kids. It was as if we had known each other forever. I had forgotten that I had Kathryn waiting on me at the coffee house.

"I must admit, I have never encountered a man like you, nor have I ever imagined that I could enjoy the company of someone such as yourself," I shared. "Not just because we are obviously complete opposites, but mostly because your personality is one that I've never seen before," I explained.

Curtis reached across the table, slowly extending his hand to me. I was nervous, and with obvious trepidation I took his hand. To my surprise, at his touch, my nerves began to calm. Curtis sensed my anxiety as he began to speak. "Mrs. Stintpindal, do you enjoy the pleasant scent of a rose?" He asked.

"Yes, I do," I responded.

"Have you ever seen a green rose with a red stem and leaf?" Curtis asked.

"No, I have not. I'm not sure that one exists either, does it?" I asked, knowing the answer to the question, but trying to understand where this conversation was going.

"A rose is a rose, and pleasant enough just as a rose. The color does not differentiate its botanical definition, it's still a rose." He continued while still holding my hand and feeling me relax in his grip. "Though you have never seen a green rose, you are familiar with the rose and are not afraid of it. MaryAnn, I am a man, like any other man, with color and characteristics of my own, but still a man, and no one to be fearful of. Would you be afraid of a green rose if it was in your hands, MaryAnn?"

I had forgotten that quickly. I had been holding hands with Curtis for quite some time now. Although I found it soothing, before responding, I released my hand from his and found my voice. "No, No I wouldn't be afraid of a green rose at all, I suppose."

"Then please take my hand and don't be afraid of me. I may be as different as a green rose, but just as pleasant as any man you could ever know. Moreover, MaryAnn, as rare a find a green rose would be, as rare a find you are," Curtis whispered.

Astonished by how well this man of the street life had articulated his metaphor, I could only respond with a nod, quietly muttering "Thank you. I've never been described as a rare find before, but you must know, Mr. Rainier, I'm a married woman."

Curtis almost choked on a glass of lemonade he was drinking; surprised at the thought that I was suggesting he was attempting to seduce me. I chimed in, "Excuse me! Do you find humor in something I said, Mr. Rainer?"

"Oh, no, not at all. MaryAnn, trust me, I am not hitting on you, I promise," Curtis responded defensively. "I was simply trying to express that my acquaintance with you happens to be an experience in my life that I could never have imagined. I also did not think a Beverly Hills socialite having lunch with a thug like myself would ever come about, as neither will a green rose with red leaf and stem. So MaryAnn, we good?" Curtis asked.

"Yes, we're good ," I said, then continued, "But now I have to ask you, Mr. Curtis Rainier, do you find me attractive?"

"Well, MaryAnn, this conversation is definitely taking a turn or two and is beginning to confuse me. I have enjoyed your company and lunch with you, but I think I better be going now. I am glad you're okay, because you seem to be a really sweet and cool little momma, and I think you have a lucky husband." Curtis then raised his hand toward the waitress and said, "Check please."

I reached out and placed my hand on top of Curtis's and said, "You did not answer my question, Mr. Rainier, do you think I am attractive?" I asked again.

"Yes, you are one of the most beautiful women I have ever met, plus you're classy and courageous, okay?" Curtis continued to speak while pulling his hand back. "Look, I've never been out with a white woman before, I especially haven't admitted to one that I found her to be attractive." Before Curtis could finish his statement, the waitress arrived with his bill for lunch. Curtis reached into his front right pocket and pulled from it a huge folded wad of money. He peeled off a hundred dollar bill, placed it within the leather booklet, and pushed away from the table. "MaryAnn, thank you for lunch, and please, be safe. It's a jungle out here, little momma," Curtis said. I was smiling but emotionally confused.

I looked at Curtis and quietly said "Thank you for

saving my life, for lunch, and your complement, Mr. Curtis Rainier, Good bye," I finished.

"Alright now," Curtis said while throwing up two fingers symbolic of the peace sign. He walked across the street where he had parked in front of a computer repair store, directly next door to the coffee shop where Kathryn and Amanda sat near the window, just as their friend had asked. As I watched Curtis enter his nice new car, I whispered aloud to myself "You are attractive and brave, Curtis."

Chapter 3

There was a knock at my bedroom door, "Mrs. Stintpindal... Mrs. Stintpindal."

Bradley, my butler, softly called out my name as he entered the lavish bedroom to awaken me. Bradley was a classic butler, a tall, trustworthy gray haired gentleman whom, of course, spoke the Queen's English, "Mrs. Stintpindal, Mr. Stintpindal is asking for you," Bradley announced, extending the cordless telephone toward me.

"Yes, dear," I said sleepily.

"MaryAnn, I just arrived here in Japan, my love, and I apologize for calling. It is awfully late here so I know it's so dreadfully early there. I only wanted you to know that I will probably be here longer than I thought, and wondered if you might reconsider joining me. I am asking, sweetheart, because it appears that I may be here longer than I suspected," Richard informed his wife.

"No, Richard, I'll be fine here, dear. You know the flight to Japan is so horribly exhausting for me, and I never have a good time when you're there on business. Besides, I have Bridge tomorrow with the ladies at the club and I would be remiss to be absent once more," I admitted.

"Very well," Richard responded, "I shall miss you dearly, and promise to return with a gift I'm sure you will treasure."

"I'm sure I will, Richard, you always impress me, dear. Would it be horribly awful if we spoke another time? I have just awoken and I am still quite exhausted."

"That's fine, MaryAnn, I understand. I'll call you soon. Get some rest, my love, sweet dreams. Goodbye," he added before disconnecting.

"Bradley, be a dear and have Rosemary bring me a cappuccino and croissant, would you?" I handed the phone to a waiting Bradley.

"Very well, Mrs. Stintpindal" the butler said, while exiting my bedroom

Though I had agreed to meet with Curtis the next time he was in town for his recording business, I had insisted he not call my phone because of my husband. Curtis had respected my request. We had not spoken since our lunch at Rousseau's, exactly eight days ago.

I had thought of him every day and obsessed at night when I was home alone. Thoughts of Curtis near made me feel safe. Richard was away on business so much, I felt as though my relationship with my husband was telecommunicative only, and since the incident, I felt a sense of insecurity and loneliness.

I decided to text Curtis for the mere purpose of saying hello, but to my surprise, Curtis immediately texted back. I hadn't expected him to reply back at such early hours, and my heart raced as I read his text message. I quickly jumped out of bed and began dressing. Moments later I was pulling one of my Mercedes out of the driveway.

I arrived at the Beverly Hilton Hotel thirty minutes late. I approached the front desk and asked the attendant if there was a message for Stephanie Coates, just as Curtis had instructed me.

"Yes, Ms. Coates, Mr. Rainier is expecting you," The attendant said while handing MaryAnn the room key card and a gift bag. "Room 238," The attendant added.

"Thank you" I said, as I nervously headed toward the elevator. I was surprised that Curtis had gone to such great lengths to keep this rendezvous so discreet. For a self-declared thug of the street life, this man sure had class, I daydreamed to myself as I entered the elevator. When the elevator doors closed, I looked into the gift bag and found a beautiful red lace Victoria Secret lingerie set, a white Victoria Secret teddy gown with white lace panties and a hand written note from Curtis that read:

Either one would make you look like something to eat, or we could keep it organic and let me have you with your bare essentials. (Smile)

w/respects,

Curtis

As I placed the note back inside the gift bag, I smiled and began to convince myself that this might be worth it after all. Curtis was indeed the spice I needed in my life right now. The elevator doors opened on the second floor and I exited and headed for room 238.

I passed the stairwell exit door and didn't notice it was slightly ajar, because Curtis was hiding there and peeking out into the hall. As soon as I passed the door, Curtis came out, sneaked up behind me, grabbed me by the arm and spun me around. Before I could scream, Curtis placed his lips on mine and began to passionately kiss a frightful MaryAnn. With my eyes wide open from fear, I had begun to melt in his grip as I realized who was stealing my kisses. Curtis continued to kiss me as my eyes closed and he guided me back into the stairwell. Once the door closed and we were alone, Curtis abruptly turned me around once more and gently pushed me against the wall. I braced myself by placing my hands on the wall as if I were going to be pat searched.

This was no airport, though, and Curtis definitely was no policeman. He was a thug and taking my emotions on a thrill ride to destinations unknown.

Curtis grabbed a fist full of my hair, and with a slight tug, pulled until my head was as far back as it could go and my face was toward my right shoulder. He had begun to aggressively suck my bottom lip as a hungry, third world child might a cold, fresh orange. I had begun to moan aloud. I could feel his free hand all over me. *My god, how many hands does he have?* I thought to myself. Curtis was kissing and sucking my face and neck, caressing my breast with his free hand. Moving down my stomach and around my waist, he made his way to my behind. I was drowning in his sea of sensuality and could not escape, Northerner did I want to. Curtis pulled my hair harder and squeezed my booty while whispering in my ear "MaryAnn, give me some of you little momma, can I have you for tonight?"

"Yes, Curtis, yes" I said. Curtis gave my hair a subtle yank.

"Oh!" I yelled out. I could feel Curtis undoing my belt, then my pants button and zipper. He pressed me harder against the wall with his body up against mine. In one swift motion he released my hair and both hands simultaneously slid down my rib cage, fingers extended as both hands plunged into my panties on both sides of my hips. My pants and panties fell to my ankles as if they were oversized to begin with.

Before I could protest, Curtis used his right hand to thrust my waist toward him. Using his left hand to encourage me to spread my legs further apart, Curtis dropped to his knees. He gently kissed my lower back, he kissed both cheeks of my buttocks, and then traced the contour of my ear with his tongue downward. Using both hands now, Curtis parted me from behind and slid his tongue from his mouth and into the moist throbbing envelope of my waiting womanhood. I had never felt pleasures of such a hypnotizing euphoria. I closed my eyes, and as Curtis licked between my thighs while firmly squeezing my buttocks, my legs began to tremble. He slid his tongue deeper within me, and applied pressure to my clitoris with his thumb. I could feel the butterflies in my stomach building up impressive pressure of warmth that would burst if he continued. He did, and so I did, bursting and screaming out for him to stop, thinking that he better not, I reached around for him to stand and take me completely.

Curtis stood, and simply said "I'll meet you in room 238." With a menacing grin, he turned and added, "don't forget your bag little momma." He was gone.

I could barely catch my breath, let alone the fact I could not believe this had happened to me. I dressed myself, grabbed my bag, and followed him to room 238, thinking to myself that I would follow him anywhere. I knew that if what I just experienced was a prelude to what may happen all night long; I would definitely never regret my night with a thug from Oakland named Curtis.

The spacious suite was dimly lit when I entered. I didn't attempt to admire the room's ambiance, I rushed to the bedroom where I heard the soft sound of music playing. When I opened the door, there he was, standing in his boxer briefs, no shirt and glistening. I took a mental picture before making my way into his arms. There was no need for small talk; we both knew what we were there for. Our approval had been solidified from the act that had taken place in the stairwell. Curtis had every intention of giving me some thug loving, the type of sex he knew only a black man of his nature could administer. He grabbed me at the fat part of my buttock and squeezed hard, pulling me up against his hardness. His lips found the right side of my neck line as he walked me backward to the bed. I kicked off my heels before our bodies introduced themselves to the mattress. Curtis wasted no time, he performed sexual acts to my body that were heart pounding, mind blowing, and unbelievable, beyond imagination. I allowed him to have me in every way he desired.

Although several hours had passed, the room remained in twilight as Curtis lounged in bed after a full morning of sex. He glanced over at me sleeping and marveled at my gorgeous profile. The bed sheets were pulled over my shoulder, slightly underneath my chin. A smooth clean line went down from the point of my shoulder to the waist, then mounded up warmly over my hip. Strands of hair layered across my cheek.

Curtis leaned over and kissed me with gentle lips. "Hmmm" I softly purred, removing the sheets from my nude body. Curtis's brown complexion glowed under the light. The look in my hazel blue eyes was a combination of a flirtatious smile and a desire to claim him as my own. It was an invasive and dominating kind of intimacy.

"Good morning honey," I whispered looking up into his eyes. I saw the thoughts in them, but his facial expression didn't give away any clues.

"Morning sleepy head," Curtis replied, scoping out my shapely figure. He leaned down without warning, gently and seductively kissing me on the navel. I moaned against my will, frustrated by how this man's touch had so much control over my body. He hoisted my legs over his shoulders after submerging his hardness into my erotic love muffin. I met my lover's every thrust. I cried out in pleasure, clawing at everything I touched. I loved the feeling of his thick long warmness inside of me. He inflamed my intensity to a much higher level of lustful desires. He took control of my arms, pried them loose of his back and gently bent them down to the mattress, then thrust himself deeper and harder into me so that his groin was pressed against mine.

He rolled over from my satisfied body; I rose up and laid my head on his chest. We enjoyed each other's company until late morning, before I announced that I had to leave. "Love, it's been an absolute pleasure. I wish I could spend more time up under you." I smiled and continued, "I must be going. We will have to do this again. I'll call you when I make it home." I kissed Curtis and departed.

Chapter 4

I pulled my luxury sedan through the security gate in front of my multi-million dollar mansion. I drove up the smooth stretch of road to the stately entrance, rolled to a stop and stepped out of the car. I was exhausted and quickly walked through the front door, heading directly to the comfort of the master bedroom. I entered my room, dropped my overnight bag and liberated myself from my clothes. *It's time for a nice long, hot bath,* I said to myself as I turned the faucet on my hot tub, allowing a steaming stream of water to flow into the tub. As I ran the bath I checked my phone. Amanda had left several messages, each one friendly but progressively more concerned. Amanda was worried because I normally call her at least once a day, every day.

I grabbed my cell phone and slipped into the hot pool of water, relaxing, and began to think about my good friend. Amanda is a nice girl, but she's a bit lonely. Tonight is our night to go out and...snap! I had an idea and dialed Curtis. Two rings, he answered, "Curtis, it's me," I said.

"Hey, lil' momma," Curtis said.

"I wanted to call to tell you I made it home okay."

"Cool."

"I was just thinking, how about dinner tonight? I got a call from my friend Amanda. Do you have a friend you could bring? We could double date, it'll be fun."

"Oh yeah? What's Amanda like?" Curtis inquired.

"Amanda is a sweet girl, an adorable person. She's just been through a divorce and is a little sour toward men, but I've noticed how lonely she is. She needs some excitement in her life."

"Yeah, I got friends, but the only one I trust with something like that is my boy Eugene, and he's locked up."

"Locked up?" I inquired.

"Yeah, in prison. He's like the brother I never had."

"Oh," I said, a bit surprised, with visions of gray concrete, cold steel bars and misery. "I guess Eugene will not be accompanying us tonight?"

"I guess you are right. I don't feel comfortable introducing your girl to any of my other friends."

"But you would have introduced her to Eugene?" I asked.

"No doubt."

"So what's so special about Eugene?"

Curtis didn't like where this conversation was going and felt defensive. He spoke highly about his boy. After he finished, I insisted that Curtis introduce Amanda to his friend Eugene. He sighed, and then decided to do just that. Why not? What will it hurt? A pen pal will be good for Eugene, Curtis thought to himself.

"I'm sure he would love to meet Amanda also." Although Eugene was locked away in a California correctional facility, if he was half the man Curtis was, he was good enough for my best friend Amanda.

I knew the biggest task would be getting Amanda to commit to corresponding with a prisoner, particular with someone she didn't know prior to his incarceration. I knew that she was lonely from the things she said during girls night out at the Spa. Us girls would get together twice a month and indulge ourselves with facials, manicures, pedicures and full body massages over a glass or two of merlot or chardonnay. This was our time to catch each other up on all the things that had been shaping our lives.

After one glass of wine Amanda seemed to come alive with emotions. Her heart had been shattered when her husband had deserted her for a man. It really tore her down to the fifth power, the idea of her now ex-husband being bisexual practically destroyed her. She undoubtedly wanted revenge to let him feel the pain, embarrassment and disrespect he caused her. But she was too proud, too independent, and too faithful to her religious beliefs, so she had walked away with nothing but a few personal possessions, her clothes, her cat, and her dignity.

Amanda was good at hiding her true feelings, and girls night out was the only way her friends could get a glimpse into her subconscious world. I was hopeful that one day a man might come along worthy of her, a man of class, personality, style, and straight as an arrow; a man with overbearing love to give. Because of course that was what Amanda needed, to be loved, sincerely, unconditionally, madly and deeply. Certainly no woman really wants to be alone without someone to love her, care for her, cherish her and be supportive and proud of her. I knew that would be my argument for why it may be good to open a line of communication with Curtis's friend Eugene. That's if she resisted. I only wanted the best for Amanda, to see her happy and excited again. If Eugene was the remedy for her happiness, then I was willing to do whatever it took to connect the dots.

Curtis met us at Isis restaurant but he didn't bring along a companion for Amanda. I introduced Amanda to him and ordered drinks. They chatted briefly about the decor of the fine restaurant before Curtis excused himself from the table and headed toward the men's room.

"Girl, what do you think of him?" I asked with excitement in my voice.

"He's definitely handsome, I can tell you that, but I don't know him yet," Amanda dulls the moment.

"You have to admit he's gorgeous. Did you see that nice hard rump he has," I bragged.

"Yeah, I guess so," Amanda replied, sounding a little down.

"He also has a best friend, named Eugene. I would like for you to meet him."

"Oh, is this what this about? You invited your boyfriend and you two decided to set me up on a blind date with his friend? At least you could have had the decency to give me a heads up so I could be looking cute and all."

"You're fine, you look stunning," I complimented.

"Where is this best friend hiding out at?" Amanda swiveled her head to scan the room for Curtis and his friend. They were nowhere in sight. She shot an inquisitive gaze toward me. I said nothing.

I waited until Amanda had two glasses of chardonnay in her before I popped the question. "Amanda, if I told you Curtis's best friend was in prison, would you still be interested in getting to know him?" I said in apprehension.

"Hell-to-the-no!" Amanda snapped suddenly. "Are you serious? I will do no such thing. Why would I want to befriend a criminal? What could a jailbird and I possibly have in common, let alone converse about?"

Amanda gazed at MaryAnn with a perplexity that was less than genuine.

"What will it hurt?" I said tentatively. "It may do your soul some good to have a pen-pal. Someone you can share your thoughts with openly and freely without being judged. If nothing more, you will have a listening ear," I said dryly, wondering if I had given a vigorous enough presentation or not.

Amanda's expression changed and her gaze grew thoughtful. There was no mistaking that she was trying to digest all the reasons for why she should consider becoming Eugene's pen-pal. She was visibly tense, but after a moment she relaxed, thoughtfully silent. Amanda smiled broadly, approvingly, as if something had finally registered within her mind. I positioned myself with familiarity on the chair, leaned back and gazed into Amanda's eyes.

Amanda smothered a sigh before it liberated her lungs. "No! No, no! What type of woman seeks a relationship with a man in prison? Oh my! Do I seem that desperate for male companionship? You think that low of me to suggest I stoop down into the gutter for a man? How dare you? Gutsy of you to fix your mouth to recommend such a thing," she snapped with venom.

My stomach jolted at the sting of her words. More shock then anything, the idea that my best friend believed that I was trying to lead her astray or thought she's desperate for a man. My heart ached for her happiness.

"Would you just consider it?"

"No!" Amanda frowned.

"Listen honey, how long have we known each other?"

"What does it matter?" Amanda snapped.

"How long?" I said firmly.

"Since grade school."

"Yes, since elementary," I said without offense. "Have I ever placed you in harm's way, physically or emotionally?"

"Of course not."

"Well, why would you think any different now? I love you from the core of my heart. I would never steer you down the wrong road. I just want to see you happy. Who would ever have thought in a million years I would date a man like Curtis. He doesn't fit the typical image of my ideal man. He would be considered morally unacceptable by my family as well. But look at me, I have found true happiness in a guy with an unconventional lifestyle. He is fun, attentive, caring, loving, spontaneous, and believe it or not, he's intelligent and God fearing. We have the most intriguing conversations. I'm telling you girl," I reminisced, smiling to myself.

"Okay enough, I get the point." Amanda smiled broadly, approvingly, as if a light flicked on somewhere in her mind from something I had said. "Okay, what will it hurt? I'll give the pen-pal thing a try. Get Eugene's information for me and I will write him or have him write me first. You can give him my P.O. Box address."

Curtis had returned to the table and apologized for his departure. He noticed from the empty glasses that the ladies had ordered another round of drinks, so he took it upon himself to order the meals; the ladies didn't mind. He entertained both of them for the rest of the night with his charm and dance moves.

Chapter 5

Curtis lay motionless, face down on his bed, sound asleep before the sound of music on his iPhone awakened him. He made an attempt to open his eyes but his heavy eyelids were weighted down by exhaustion from the sex sequel he participated in with MaryAnn. His body was now feeling the after effects. He moaned in agitation, wiping saliva from his chin with his left hand. He then reached over to the night stand and blindly groped around for the phone. *Who in the hell could this be calling me*, he thought as he fumbled around in a search to locate the phone, knocking over his wad of hundred dollar bills onto the floor. "Hello" He grunted into the palm size iPhone. A computerized recording began, he listened for a few seconds before realizing it was a collect call from his best friend Eugene, who was housed at the Valley State Prison in Chowchilla, California. Curtis didn't bother to listen to the entire recording, he knew the formalities quite well. *"The man I need to talk to,"* he mouthed to no one but himself, thumbing the touch screen to except the call.

"What's up, bruh?" Curtis said excitedly to hear from Eugene

"Shit! Another one like the other one. Tired of being in prison," Eugene replied.

"I feel you. Your time is coming, just stay focused. Bruh, I been meaning to write you a letter because there is so much I need to talk to you about and for some reason I can never remember when we talk on the phone. First of all, I have to say me and the family miss you. Your nephew says hi. Your nieces keep asking when you're coming out. Frankly, I don't know what to tell them; I just keep saying soon. Anyways, I'm glad to finally be on top of my game. Thank God for that. Don't know why the Lord keeps on blessing me but I am grateful for his grace and mercy. Looks like he is gonna bless me with a new business opportunity that might do very well, seeing as how there is no establishment like the one I'm looking into. But I been having some stagnation on rushing into this thing alone because of some choices I've made to free up some time for you and Colton.

"I don't remember if I told you or not, but I had to set aside my business with my record label and pursuing my music because I didn't know that this nonprofit thing would consume so much of my time and energy. Now before you get upset, please understand I am not complaining because I know how important it is to you and Colton. I understand what it's like to be in your shoes, so I know how important it is to be supportive and to be hands and feet for a man behind the wall. You my family and Colton has proven to be a pretty solid guy. I never expressed this to him, so keep this to yourself, but I like his style. He is more like you and I than any of the niggas that we hang with. He has that business fire and that hungry spirit like us. He doesn't come off as a dead weight, so I think we'll do well chasing paper with him too. But like I said, don't get upset but there are some obstacles that I'm finding myself confronted with that I did not foresee some time ago."

"Bruh, what are you talking about?" asked a confused Eugene.

"It's really nothing, just forget I mentioned it. But look, I have someone I want you to meet, a female, are you interested?"

"Who is this woman? How do you know her? What she looks like? Does she know I'm locked up?"

"Hold up, bruh, let me answer one question at a time. First of all, this woman is a friend of my new tender-roni. I'ma have to sit down and write to tell you about that. Anyways, she has a friend name Amanda and asked me to introduce her to one of my friends. So bruh, you came to mind. I don't know too much about her but from what I was told by my girl MaryAnn, she's good people. Divorced, no kids, forty-eight years old, and she has her own business. That's all I know about her. I will try to get a picture to send you so you can see how she looks. Looks shouldn't matter to you anyways. So what's up? You want to holla' at baby or what?"

"Nah, I'm cool. I have too many other things on my plate right now. I can't be wasting my time."

"Nigga! What you have better to be doing than getting at a female? Don't tell me you scared at getting at a woman?"

"Being scared don't have anything to do with it. I just don't have time for all the games and lies. If she wants to write a guy in prison she might be damaged, you know? I'm cool with all the drama that comes along with a scarred woman."

"Bruh, give baby a try. You can't think everyone is the same because others have treated you bad or let you down since you been in prison. Everyone is not the same. You have to start trusting someone one day. Look, my girl MaryAnn gave me an address on baby to give you. She insisted that I have you to drop her friend a line or two, so get a pen and paper and write this down."

"Aight, what is it?"

Curtis gave Eugene the address before the phone call ended. He knew that his boy would write Amanda a letter. He smothered the iPhone with one of the goose feather pillows that rested on the bed and reclaimed his position before he was interrupted of his sleep.

Chowchilla, California

An indecisive Eugene hung up the phone when the fifteen minute phone time allotted for inmate calls was up. He debated whether or not he should call Curtis back to inquire more into this pen-pal love connection Curtis and his girlfriend MaryAnn were attempting to make between him and Amanda. The very thought of meeting someone who could become a special part of his life had his mind racing in many directions. His curiosity entertained the desire for more answers to his unspoken questions.

Excitement was plastered on his face and in his steps as he strolled away from the phone booth back to his cell. The strong sense of loneliness he felt seemed to have found another victim to taunt. He stood in front of his living quarters, cell 22, with his hand on the door handle awaiting the correctional officer to electronically unlock it.

Eugene was greeted at the entrance by a smiling, playful Raul, one of his five cellmates who he nicknamed Felipe for no apparent reason other than he felt the name fit him. Felipe is Hispanic, the entertainment of the cell, a big kid at heart who goes to sleep and wakens with a smile and ready to joke around. All in all he is a good hearted person, always willing to help others in need. Standing behind him at one of the porcelain sinks nursing a hot-pot full of boiling water is Felipe's mini-me, Jump-in-Derrick, the nickname given to him by Eugene because he was always jumping into their conversations without an invitation. Jump-in-Derrick is harmless, a little touched, but funny, and always has an outrageous story to tell about something that has happened to him, sometimes involving animals he has "squared off with," it may it be fiction or not, you have to decide.

Kevin and Jerry were engaged in their daily rituals. Jerry is a quiet, respectful old school convict of Mexican descent. He is assigned to a lower bunk in the dorm and deeply involved in drawing another one of his portraits. He was a professional artist and managed to sell his works for premium prices, allowing for him to get the things he needed in prison.

Kevin is African American, black as coal, with a oversized shaved head and a huge mustache. Kevin kept his Hulk Hogan style handle bar mustache well manicured. He kept a palm comb in one hand and a bible in the other. He was quick to dive into a mirror, pull out his comb and sculpt any unruly section of his stash when he felt it necessary. However, he spent the majority of his time quietly reading his bible. He was so quiet you wouldn't even know he was in the cell.

Then there was Colton, AKA Commando Nerd. Colton is a clean shaven white dude who looked like a professor or executive, but in fact was a high steel ironworker before winding up in prison. His previous life was filled with outdoor activity but he managed to adapt to the boredom and confinement of prison life through scholarly pursuits. He spent most his time quietly studying. He had completed a college degree and often encouraged and helped other inmates with their education. He and Eugene had similar perspectives on life and the way one should be "doing time." They both believed in living with purpose and preparing for their return to society. They were close friends.

Eugene beelined to his own bunk as usual. He was not burdened with a bunkie, so he used the empty top bunk as a writing surface. He dug into his locker and removed two color folders and set them on the metal surface. He opened the green folder, removed a sheaf of blank white paper, and closed the folder. He then opened the blue folder and shuffled through its contents. He pondered on one of the documents for a moment before removing it. He gazed over at Felipe as he attempted to gather his thoughts. He had his pen in hand and paper in front of him, but his unspoken words were lost in space. Eugene was clueless; he hadn't written an introduction letter to a lady in years. He didn't know how he should start it. He made several attempts, but quickly crumpled them up and shoved them into a pile. His letter writing campaign wasn't panning out as he hoped. He reached back into his locker and removed his portable CD player and stack of CDs. He shuffled through the stack before stopping at one of his favorite R&B artists. He removed the CD from its case and secured it in the prison approved clear see-through CD player. He pushed play before thumbing the volume button and placing the head phones over his ears. That was all it took to get Eugene in the mood to compose a letter. The music put him in a zone far away from the reality of being incarcerated.

When he finished, Eugene proofread his letter before folding it in thirds. He inserted it into a white Valley State Prison indigent envelope. The envelopes are provided to indigent inmates postage paid, however Eugene wasn't indigent, just thrifty. He could trade a single stamp or a Top Ramen noodles soup on the inmate black market for five of the state indigent envelopes and the mailroom would send them out just the same.

He thought against using such an envelope because he didn't want to make a bad impression, but he was unsure his prospective pen-pal would respond back so he decided to save his stamp and use an indigent envelope. Eugene had been in prison over a decade and learned that every little bit counts, and that disappointment of family and friends was common for all inmates. So he was not hopeful about this opportunity to meet a new friend. He slipped the letter into the outgoing mail slot on his way out to the exercise yard and hoped for the best.

Chapter 6

Thinking of Curtis had me floating on cloud nine as I prepared myself for the daily activities at work. He seemed to have that effect over me. It had been several days since we had spoken and I found myself obsessing over thoughts of him. I took up a seat in front of my computer and made another studied gesture past the screen before rising to my feet. I walked toward the conference room to observe the large unfamiliar object I noticed on the table. To my surprise, it was an elegant massive gift basket filled with a variety of French chocolate truffles, pretzels, claws, toffee cookies, dark chocolate drops and squares, sea salt olive oil crackers, olive red pepper tapenade roasted garlic and onion dip mix, garlic crackers, dried fruit and nuts, Italian milk chocolate pralines, cappuccino chocolate chip cookies, smoked salmon and many other goodies. But what caught my full attention was not the pink envelope that featured my name leaning against the bottle of Dom Perignon, but the single leafy green rose placed in a clear crystal vase.

I carefully extracted the card from the envelope and began reading its contents.

"This rare green rose reminded me of your beauty and exceptional personality. Please accept it as a token of my appreciation of you. Please join me for lunch at LAX airport 11:45 am today. I'll meet you in the lobby, sweet thoughts, Curtis."

I secured the card back in its envelope and placed it

how I had found it. Puzzled, I wondered where he may have obtained a green rose. If it wasn't for the fact I was holding it in my hand, I would never imagine a rose of such color existed. It seemed as though the rose was beckoning me to smell its fragrance, so I leaned closer as my nose entered its personal space and claimed its exotic scent.

"Ah, this man is too good to be true," I expressed to myself.

I had forgotten about my obligations to my job at the foundation. My mind was racing back and forth over whether or not I should go change outfits. I was becoming a bit frantic. *Should I leave my hair up or lay it down? Where in the LAX does he plan to have lunch and why the LAX airport? Should I call him to confirm my acceptance of his lunch invitation? I probably should. That would be the appropriate thing to do*, I assured myself before rushing to make the call.

Amanda had a long tiresome day at work. Fatigue was motivating her to hurry straight home. She was ready to recline in the comfort of the hot massaging water of her Jacuzzi. She stopped at the post office to pick up her mail on the way. She ran in, ran right back out and jumped into her burgundy Navigator SUV. A brand new model with smoke tinted windows and chrome rims. She sank into the deep leather seat before pulling off.

Amanda fumbled with the electronic buttons of the gadget on her visor, the security gate slowly opened and she drove through the entrance of the gated community. The houses were obviously track homes as they were all built similarly and painted the same color. The front yard had a single tree in the middle of a figure eight design patch of grass surrounded by gravel, Amanda's yard was neat and clean with shrubs of rose bushes lining the house barrier giving the illusion of a small fence enclosing the yard, leaving the three car garage exposed. The red, yellow, pink and white rose bushes decorated the property with a vision of luxury and filled the air with a beautiful aromatic smell, a beauty to be adored.

The neighborhood was so peaceful and innocent. The only sound that could be heard was the low humming of wind milling air conditioner fans installed on the side of every house. Amanda had pulled up in front of the house and parked at an angle partially in the driveway. She stretched her arms over her head and then let out a yawn as she stepped out of the truck. She admired the view of her rose bushes and inhaled deeply their fragrance mingled with the night air before keying the locks. She could hear the two dogs shuffling toward the front door. She entered and thumbed an eight digit code into the security system number pad. Several locks clicked and the sound of a chain loosely dangled up against the door as it closed. She gently clawed the top of the heads of her trained German Sheppard's.

Amanda hustled upstairs to the master bedroom and began preparing for a bath. She placed two fragrant bath beads into the Jacuzzi tub as it filled with water, then she lit the half melted scented candles around the tub and blew out the match she held between her fingers. A faint trail of smoke rose from the match. She stopped at the mirror to admire her beauty and rearrange her hair before inspecting the size of her breasts. She noticed the growth and the decline of her once erect twins. She knew there was nothing she could do to stop the force of gravity other than find a push up bra to support them better. She flirted with herself a second longer before deciding to go through the mail. To her surprise there was a letter from Eugene. Her heart pounded against her chest. Fear and excitement were mingling with her emotions as she liberated the contents from the envelope. The letter gave off a pleasant scent and was surprisingly composed with beautiful handwriting that was not common in this computer age. She admired the uniqueness and the effort he put forth in his approach. She began reading it with attentive eyes.

SHOOTER: Eugene Weems T-40463
                 P.O. Box 92
                 Chowchilla, CA 93610
TARGET: Amanda Aniston
AIM: Your mind, heart, soul and hand in
               Friendship

Dear Amanda,

Please understand this is not my usual way of acquainting myself with a lady I am not familiar with. So please bare with me as I navigate my way around this approach clumsy-like, hoping I say or do something well enough to merit a response from you. MaryAnn suggested that I compose this introduction letter, so here I am taking a leap of faith in hoping to meet a new friend.

So, Amanda, if I could compose something so real and of so much substance that I could change your perspective of a man in prison, would you be woman enough to admit it? If I could change your mind about the abilities of a man from beyond these walls, would you let me? Well?

First of all, the following is for a mature woman, for the non-judgmental, for the compassionate, patient, understanding, and forgiving woman. Could this woman be you? I'm sure you would like answers to your unspoken thoughts and yet to be asked questions such as, why am I in prison? What am I doing to prevent coming back to prison once I'm out? Do I believe in God?

Amanda, I was a professional kick boxer who was manipulated into a situation that ended with me in prison for a jewelry store heist that netted over one million dollars. In accepting responsibility for my own actions, I would not include others who got away. I have been in custody for over fourteen years already. Now that I'm close to coming home, I'm ready to start fresh. I can only do that if the rest of the world accepts me as a new man. I'm hoping you can be one person that can see past my misfortune.

The age difference just may be something you're uncomfortable with. Honestly, I never asked MaryAnn your age. I was stuck on your youthful beauty of the photo Curtis sent me. Age doesn't matter to me. If it matters to you, can I ask you why? Do you want an old man or a young man that can and will meet all of your needs? I don't believe love gets old. If it does, then it shows me I've still so much to learn.

I have begun doing as much positive and good in my life to create balance for the errors of my past ways, and yes, I do believe in God. I'm no religious fanatic, though. This prison life has changed me for the better. I've learned so much and I can offer you an abundance of truth and honesty, if only you would be willing to put even a smidgeon of faith in me. I dare not disappoint. Let's just say, I promise to be fragile with your heart if you let me hold it, or even as a friend, let me learn your smile honestly, let me get to know you some.

I need a friend who understands that even an intelligent gentleman such as myself could and actually does truly exist in a place you would least expect to find a gem. Should I not be confident in myself because at one point in my life I allowed circumstances to make decisions for me? Or should I pick myself up, shake the dust off and share myself with the world once more? See, you are a smart woman, and if you're still reading, I submit that you are a mature reader and woman of equal caliber who I could probably enjoy intelligent dialog with, sharing ideas, exploring possibilities, and overall traveling the journeys that pen and paper, phone conversations, and maybe even visits could take us. Welcome to my sanctuary of inner trust, where you'll be safe to share with me anything you wish and my life being an open book is yours for the browsing.

By the way, I am the author of "United We Stand," "The

Other Side of the Mirror" and "Prison Secrets." A few of life's accomplishments I am proud of. I would love to know more about you and allow you the same opportunity vice versa. Interested?

I know I'm laying a lot down in my first letter, but hey, I've been a little lonely lately. Just being honest. I'm glad to make your acquaintance, though. I am Eugene Weems and you just made a friend. Hope you write back. It would be nice to have my name called at mail call. It also would be nice if I could see your pretty face even if it's a picture. I'm really a nice and compassionate guy, just a bit nervous about this kind of start is all.

I'll be waiting to hear from you.

Sincerely, your new friend,

Eugene

Chapter 7

It was a warm sunny California day and I met Curtis as requested. I was so excited I hardly noticed the busy traffic in LAX when I saw Curtis leaning against a kiosk. His cool dapper demeanor stood out in stark contrast to the chaos of the airport. I was drawn to him by some magnetic force of nature, and gave him an affectionate hug.

"Are you ready?" he asked.

"Ready?" I inquired curiously.

"Yeah, are you ready to go?"

"Go where?"

"You'll see, it's a surprise. You trust me, right?"

"Sure. Why? Should I be concerned?"

Curtis smiled down at me and took my hand in his, then led the way to a terminal for private jets. We walked right through the departure area, boarded one of the aircraft and took up comfortable seats in the spacious cabin. Evidently, we were the only passengers on this flight. Without warning the jet began moving faster and faster down the stretch of runway until we were swept away.

Las Vegas, Nevada

The private jet roared to a landing at McCarran International Airport, Las Vegas, Nevada. Taxiing along the tarmac, the sleek aircraft slowly turned and rolled to a separate facility just north of the main terminal. McCarran was bustling with jets and service personnel going about their daily routines.

We disembarked and I immediately felt the notorious furnace blast of Las Vegas heat. The striking heat only added to my excitement as I looked out and saw a stretch pearl white limousine awaiting our arrival. The chauffer climbed out of his seat when he noticed Curtis and I depart the plane and ceremoniously opened the door for us. Before entering the luxury vehicle, I took in the delicate smell of roses on the wind. Curtis had arranged for green rose pedals to grace the pitch black tarmac. It was a stunning scene.

I watched the chauffeur returned to the driver's seat and carefully maneuver us out of the bustling airport and down east Hacienda Avenue to Las Vegas Boulevard. To my surprise, we pulled up to the entrance of the glorious Mandalay Bay Resort and Casino. Our chauffeur rushed out and opened the door before the casino's bell hop made his move. We exited the vehicle, disappointing the bell hop with our lack of baggage.

Curtis gently took my hand and led me into the casino. It was breathtaking; the reflective gold facade was too much to take in at one glance as I was being navigated to our destination. China Grill the sign read over the high end restaurant. It was obvious that one must have reservations to dine there. Curtis must have been a regular because the waitress recognized him as we entered and seated us immediately.

The waitress paused and shot a smile at Curtis, he nodded faintly. She swiveled fast on her feet and was lost somewhere in the stainless steel and clatter of the restaurant's kitchen. I was mesmerized by the illuminated domed ceiling of the establishment. The high-tech 3-D computerized graphics depicted shooting stars, planets, and all kinds of astronomical phenomena, it was astonishing. The night sky scene set the mood as if we were having lunch under the moon and stars. How amazing, absolutely breathtaking.

I was so captivated by the visuals that I hadn't noticed the waitress return with the appetizer and vanish once again. I love Saki-cured salmon rolls, how did Curtis know? I wanted to ask, but decided not to. I sampled the appetizer more than once. The waitress found her way back, but this time balancing several entrees on her arm and hands. She kept glancing into Curtis's eyes as she worked. He was very casual, but quiet. Why I was feeling jealous and overly protective of Curtis? Maybe it was the unspoken communication and looks they exchanged with one another. My emotions were getting the best of me. I wanted to know what was going on. So I just asked bluntly, "Do you two know each other?" A harmless question I supposed. No one responded. It seemed as if my question had fallen on deaf ears. I gazed over at Curtis and he shot me a smirk. I turned my attention to the waitress who was liberating her hands of entrees.

"Excuse me miss, how do you know Curtis?" I'd asked a question of unforgivable intrusion.

"She..." Curtis attempted to speak but I put a finger decisively against his lips.

"He's my boss," The waitress offered and added "Sir, is there anything else I can get you?"

"No, this will be fine, Michelle, thank you," he said. And she turned on her heels and strolled off. Boss... Michelle...this picture wasn't adding up. I normally wouldn't care either way, but I was becoming emotionally invested in this man. My dream didn't include any other woman, only me. Curtis noticed the frustration within my face. He nodded his recognition and reached over to touch my hand to assure me that everything was okay, before he displayed his handsome smile.

"I took the liberty to order lunch for us," Curtis

announced.

I eyed all the different entrees. They looked so delicious, but it was too much for two people. "This is way too much food," I said.

"I thought it would be nice to sample different dishes so I can learn your favorites," then stretched out an arm with a fork in his hand, "Try this babe, it is shanghai lobster with ginger, curry, and crispy spinach." I mouthed the fork full of food. It was delicious as promised. My favorite dish was the sizzling whole fish in Chinese black-bean and red chili sauce. For dessert we had chocolate cake with raspberry caulis, and warm fudge walnut tarts. I told myself I would pay the Family Fitness Center a two hour visit once I made it back to California.

Curtis was a man who knew how to set the mood for any occasion. I have never been flown to another state just to have lunch. I couldn't wait to tell Amanda and the girls about this when we have our next girl's day at the spa. This man was perfectly prepared, romantic, and well diverse between the sheets. I was ready to please him in so many ungodly ways that the steam from my kitty had moistened my panties. I moved closer, straddled him, my lips automatically entered his personal space. What beautiful full lips, so voluptuous and inviting. The remembrance of the many orgasmic pleasures those very lips provided only intensified the raging hunger between my thighs. I felt his hands slowly moving up my skirt. The throbbing bulge beneath me swelled with pride. I was convinced this episode was about to be one of those "what happens in Vegas stays in Vegas" moments but Curtis reclaimed his hands before smacking me on the rear and hurried me out the restaurant.

"We going to be late, we have a plane to catch," he said as we rushed to the limo. Our chauffeur must have noticed us as we exited Mandalay Bay Resort and Casino, because he was holding the passenger door open for us. We stepped in and moments later we were en route to our destination.

We raced back to McCarran in record time and made our way through the airport crowds. This time Curtis took me to a different terminal. I assumed on such short notice, he had to get a return flight on a different airline.

He led me to the Pan Am check-in line. "Pan Am?" I asked inquisitively.

"Yeah, I'm not ready to go home just yet. How 'bout you?" He asked.

"No, I guess not, but what do you mean? Where do you want to go, what do you have in mind?" I say, a bit confused.

"The Bahamas."

"What?" assuming I heard him wrong.

"The Bahamas," he said again patiently.

"Wait a minute, the Bahama *islands,* down near Florida, all the way across the country, in the Caribbean?"

"Well, technically they're in the Atlantic, but yeah, the Bahama *islands. W*hat do you think? Wanna go? I reserved some tickets."

Wow, I thought, *really? I didn't pack for that. In fact I didn't pack for anything. I thought we were just going to lunch. What was I going to wear? But what the hell, why not?*

"Have you been there? Do you know where to go? I mean, that's a long way to go. Do you know where to stay and everything?" I asked, a little manic, and then more importantly, "I don't have any clothes for a trip like that."

"Look, don't worry baby," he slipped his arms around me. " I have everything taken care of, it will be fun," he whispered in my ear.

"Okay," I whisper back. Feeling reassured, I gave him a light kiss on the cheek and we walked down the boarding ramp and onto the plane, then off into the bright blue Las Vegas sky.

New Providence Island, Bahamas.

The first class private jet flight across country was made all the more enjoyable with an in-flight movie, glass of wine, and renewal of my membership in the mile high club. The three-hour flight direct to New Providence Island passed by quickly. Before I knew it, I was in a private car being whisked away down a freshly paved road across the tropical island. We traveled a beautiful scenic route along the ocean via West Bay Street and caught a colorful sun setting to the west.

I took a well deserved nap on the flight, so I was fresh and wide awake when we arrived at the marina in Nassau Harbor. It was a warm tropical evening as we walked toward the marina's many boats, rhythmically rising and falling with the current, woven steel rigging lines gently clinking against their metal masts like giant wind chimes.

Curtis took my hand and led me over the little bridge connecting the docks to the shore and down the ramp to the marina's yacht slips. There, tied alongside the outer main dock, was a gleaming pearl white and gold trim cutter rig schooner. The modern sailing vessel was equipped with burnished bronze wenches and cleats, clean white running rigging ropes and shining gold tackle and fixtures. The yacht was a thing of beauty, both functional and luxuriant at the same time, a vehicle fit for royalty.

As Curtis and I approached the steps leading aboard, a tall light skinned black man in a neatly pressed all white captain's uniform complete with gold buttons and skippers cap appeared seemingly out of nowhere. In one smooth motion the captain stepped to the thin safety rails which outlined the elegant yacht, unhooked a short piece of safety cable and said, "Good evening Mr. Rainier, so good to see you again sir, please, come aboard."

"How are you Mr. James?" Curtis asked with a broad, friendly smile. It was evident that the men knew each other and appeared as though they had previously spent some good times together.

"I'm doing good but not as good as you, with such a beautiful lady on your arm," said the captain.

"I've been very fortunate lately, is she ready to sail?" Curtis asked as we stepped aboard.

"Of course. You know how we do it. We stay ready, so we don't have to get ready," Mr. James said as he clipped the safety cable back in place.

"Right on, right on" Curtis chuckled.

I stepped across the spacious stern area and began to feel a sense of adventure I had not felt in a long time. I am no sailor but I looked around the yacht and noted the teak decking and gunwales, stained exotic hardwood rudder post, wheel, and sophisticated design of the exterior areas. This boat was first class and ready for some serious open water cruising.

Mr. James shouted something that sounded like "shove off" down into the interior of the sailboat. Curtis and I take seats on the all white bench cushions and notice a hatch in the bow section pop-up. A figure appearing to be a teenage boy in a white shirt and white board shorts quickly leapt off the fore area of the boat and landed smoothly on the dock. He immediately began loosening the yacht's mooring lines from the dock cleats and gently pushed the hull away from the dock, tossing the lines up to the deck. Captain James throttled up the already idling inboard diesel engine and the magnificent vessel began to pull away from its moorings. Just in time, the young crewman jumped back into the stern of the boat, smiling.

"Hey hey Junior" Curtis said. "Boy you're getting big" he added. Looking at Captain James he continued, "Your boy must have grown a foot since I last saw him, when? Last summer? Damn, what are you, like six foot now?"

"Something like that." Junior said.

"Yeah, it's all the sunshine and water we have down here, mon, he shot up like a coconut sprout," The captain explained.

I noticed a slight Jamaican accent to Mr. James' voice and together with all these smiling faces, I began to feel like I was on a real vacation. I could even hear a faint kettle drum with a reggae beat as the boat motored past the resort bar on its way out of the marina.

Junior moved forward and deftly unhooked the mainsail ties from around the mainsail carefully furled along the booms. As the vessel glided along and turned out of Nassau harbor into the open sea. "Looks like we have a wind this evening, Curtis," Captain James said, then turned the wheel slowly to starboard, pointing the bow straight into the wind, and throttled down the humming diesel engine.

My excitement turned to trepidation as I realized I had never sailed before, not in real life and never at night. I'd seen movies and been on my father's power yacht but that's not the same as this. I leaned into Curtis and snuggled up. Curtis was calm and relaxed; he had been here before and was thoroughly enjoying the ride.

Junior quickly untied some rigging on the mast and began hoisting up the mainsail, tied off the stay, then hoisted the fore mainsail, followed by the jib sails. It seemed that Mr. James was in control of the natural world as he turned the wheel just a little more and the wind began to blow over the portside. On cue Curtis helped crew the boat by reaching over with one hand, wrapped the starboard self tailoring wench and pulled the sheet line taut.

Whump, whump, *was that thunder?* I thought to myself. I look up at the billowing sails reaching into the night as they filled with wind. Whump, whump the white canvas sails tightened against the moonlight sky and filled to capacity, pulling the sheet lines even tighter, the boat heeled over to starboard and established an even keel.

We sailed into the channel past the colonial beach lighthouse, down the length of Paradise Island, and out into the tropical, blue Bahamian waters. "Where are we going?" I asked curiously.

"We just gonna go out around this spot here," so familiar with his surroundings he thumbed the route as if he were giving directions to the corner store, "They call it," Curtis paused for effect... "Rose Island." Smiling and laughing, I realized the thoughtfulness and preparation Curtis had put into this wonderful little cruise.

Thoroughly enjoying the trip, after awhile I noticed a low lying classic strip of island off the port bow well lit by the full moon. Just as I began to point to the land, little James comes up the set of steps descending into the interior of the world class sailing yacht. He holds a silver tray piled high with delectable looking appetizers, each one speared with fancy decorative toothpicks.

Captain James and crew disappear, leaving the two of us alone. The private cruise ship was underway and as it silently glided along, I was amazed. I was so excited I needed to stand up and have a look around. The majesty of a seventy-two foot yacht cruising under full sail in the open ocean was overwhelming. My eyes welled with tears and pride. Curtis may be a thug who lived the street life, but this was unbelievable! No one had ever taken me away like this. A true Caribbean cruise, with class, and it was just beginning.

I started to get curious about the inside of the yacht. *What's it like in there?* I thought to myself. Curtis noticed me looking over toward the entrance, "Want to check it out?" he asked, reading my mind.

"Yeah, let's go inside," I said, excited.

We entered the interior of the yacht, stepping down a short flight of stairs. I was surprised at the opulence of its cabin area. Lavishly appointed, it looked like a penthouse made for a prince or something, with clean white carpet, comfortable leather cushioned redwood furniture, recessed lighting, huge flat screen television, state of the art entertainment system, and down the hall through a glass door I could see what appeared to be a bubbling full size Jacuzzi.

A small "L" shaped chart table tucked away to one side of the common area was the only furnishing that gave away the yacht's functional purpose. It was neat and squared away but filled with modern digital navigational and communications equipment. A small state room with a gold placard on the door labeled "Captain" assured me of where the captain must have disappeared to. It appeared that the fantastic yacht could be controlled from within the office.

After looking around a bit, Curtis took my hand and led me aft to the master cabin. As I entered I realized the cabin must take up the entire stern area of the boat. It was as spacious as a first rate resort suite, king size bed with an assortment of pillows, designer sheets and full shower and bath adorned with shining gold fixtures.

Carefully laid out on the comforter of the huge mattress was a full set of new women's clothing, lingerie, and luxurious thick white bath robes and towels. Next to the bed on the night stand was a woven basket overflowing with hand towels, loofas, perfumes, lotions and assorted beauty and hygiene items. On a carefully crafted glass coffee table sat another basket filled with what may have been every kind of fruit in the world, I could see oranges, apples grapes, cherries, mangos, kiwis and various melons hiding in the deep basket.

With the extravagance of the room my curiosity got the best of me, I couldn't help but explore the closet, restroom and shower areas, which I discovered were all filled with first class accoutrement. The clothes were all the right sizes and styles. It was the perfect lovers nest. Curtis had pulled out all the stops.

All the excitement and fresh ocean air was making me sleepy but I still had enough energy left to take Curtis's hand and lead him to the bed. I wanted to thank him for all of his thoughtfulness and expense. But Curtis had his own idea and gave me a warm embrace.

Curtis's kiss was laced with a sentiment of an erotic touch that thundered a tingle through my veins. I inhaled deeply the freshness of his breath, trapping its sweetness in my lungs as our tongues slowly cuddled.

I attempted to take in the scenery of the richly adorned suite while marinating in the muscular arms of such a handsome, tall, honey complexion of a man, whose muscular frame was confined within a pinstriped tailor made suit that complemented the ostrich skin boots. I imagine they had to be a size between eleven and a half or twelve.

I couldn't help but recall the pleasures that he had repeatedly been giving me between the sheets and various other places. Immediately I felt overwhelmed with a tingling sensation between my thighs. My desire for Curtis could only be measured in exponential form and that in itself falls far short of its true magnitude.

Each time I gazed into his eyes. I was drawn into the farthest reaches of his mind's inner world. There, I found a land of compassion, understanding, love, affection, attentiveness and endless mind blowing sex and some good fortune. I imagined myself as one of its inhabitants.

There I stood in his embrace in an exotic white silk bathrobe. My inviting pose exposed the black panties and matching bra I was wearing. Our tongues parted their separate ways. He reached out a hand and with his index finger softly traced my succulent lips then bee lined his way down my bosom to my stomach, past my navel and stopped at the pulsating kitten between my legs. Without warning his hand slid back the curtain of my panties and his index finger penetrated my sweetness.

I took on such a wonderful pleasure from his finger entertaining my most precious gem. He knelt down as if he was about to propose to me. I didn't attempt to stop him. He gripped my hips and pulled me closer to his face. I felt his lips at my kitten and tongue searching for a way in.

I now felt as if I was about to faint, but he went on pleasantly lapping at my clitoris, scrambling with ways to stroke, suck and caress it with his tongue. Suddenly an explosion went off inside of me as I gyrated my pelvis on his face and almost lose my footing.

He managed to get me off a rapid round before the warm sticky wetness streamed down his face. What a treat this gentleman had provided. I felt intuitively that a great and disturbing change was taking place, which I recklessly promised myself would never happen in a million years. I was falling in love with a man I knew my family and social circle would never accept.

The night passed in blissful, deep sleep. As I woke, I noticed the gorgeous colors of an approaching dawn through one of the yachts bronze portholes. It was as though a brilliant painting hung on the bulkhead. I roused myself up from the warm cozy sheets excited, but careful not to wake a still sleeping Curtis, and slipped on one of the silk nightgowns that had been laid out for me. I stepped out through the cabin door, padded through the quiet hall and up the stairs to the gently rolling deck. I was surprised to find we were under sail. The skipper and crew had anchored the boat in a little cove during the night. I was busy with Curtis, but I saw our anchorage through the moonlight shortly before drifting off to sleep. I had assumed we were still in the cove but now as I looked out over the rolling blue swells I could see we were traveling toward the low lying city edifices of Nassau in the distance.

I had the deck all to myself and enjoyed the fresh cool morning breeze. As I looked out over the sea in the calm stillness of the breaking dawn, I began to feel a kind of peace I'd not felt in a long time, maybe ever.

The glorious vessel soon sailed back to Nassau harbor; we disembarked and were on a plane shortly thereafter. The flight back to Los Angeles was a blur. I slept all the way and found myself kissing Curtis goodbye in the LAX departure area. After our wonderful getaway I hated to leave him but he said he had some pressing business. I understood, but wondered when I would see him again.

My husband had returned early from Japan with thoughts of spending some quality time with his wife. He felt it would be a welcome surprise since he didn't have the leisure of downtime to enjoy my company. As I came through the door, Bradley the butler motioned in an attempt to warn me of my husband's return, but I was coasting in on cloud nine and failed to notice the gesture.

I navigated through the luxuriant home toward my bedroom. My heart and mind were still held captive to the sea of emotions and fantasies I experienced with my lover. I liberated my feet from the high heels before entering the double doors of my sanctuary. To my surprise Richard was relaxing, sprawled out across the bed, dressed only in his boxer shorts. He rose to his feet when I entered. Panic suddenly flooded my thoughts, my heartbeat seemed to stop somewhere in oblivion.

"Hello honey, are you surprised to see me?" Richard asked, gently pulling me into his arms. I was stunned, I couldn't find my voice. I was more than surprised, I was in total disbelief. *What in the world is he doing home?* was the only thought my mind could muster.

"Honey, are you okay?" He guided my face toward his, intending to kiss my lips, but he was rejected. Finding my voice, "I'm not in the mood." I liberated myself from his embrace and stormed away into the bathroom, slamming the door behind me. I quickly undressed and stepped into the shower allowing the warm water to introduce itself to my body.

I broke down in tears; my heart was torn between two men. I truly loved Richard but the intimate desire was no longer there, the very touch of my husband's hand was irritating. I enjoyed Curtis's company, the attentions he showed me, and the sex was like icing on the cake. But the reality of my life began to creep in and I knew that something had to give.

I decided my marriage was more important than this exciting new affair I was indulging in. I began to realize I needed to close this chapter in my life before it ruined my marriage. I decided to call Curtis to meet him at Starbucks so I could break the news to him.

Chapter 8

Eugene hadn't heard back from Amanda in a week, he was wondering if she had received his letter or maybe it was lost in the mail. He decided to write another letter. He reached for his pen and paper and began composing a letter to Amanda. Once he was finished he took a moment to read it back to himself.

SHOOTER: Eugene Weems T-40463
            P.O. Box 92
            Chowchilla, CA 93610
TARGET: Amanda Aniston
AIM: Your mind, heart, soul and hand in
            friendship

Hello Amanda,

Hope all was well and you are in wonderful health. I'm a believer that MaryAnn made an attempt to introduce us for a reason, believing that we share a common interest and some compatibility or she wouldn't have requested that I write you a letter. So I'm assuming you either misplaced my address or never received my letter, or just have been too busy with the daily rituals of living life. But I'm doing everything I can to convince myself it was not something I said or did between the moment you decided to allow me to write you and the moment you received my first letter that turned you off about me completely.

If you're extra guarded, let me share with you a bit about me. Of course, a saint I ain't. I know ain't isn't proper grammar, but again, I'm just being down to earth honest since this was my last attempt at trying to know you. I feel you deserve to know everything about the man you'll choose to grant a personal invite into your life or even the man you'll choose to ignore. In case you choose to ignore me instead, at least I'll know I was sincere in my approach and you can hopefully still appreciate my honesty and surrender. Why am I alone in prison, a handsome guy like myself? Well, karma, I suppose, what goes around comes around. Yeah, there was a time I broke a heart or two. I've had girlfriends and played the field before, even though I had Ms. Right once, but when I tried to be Mr. Right, all that I did prior to finding who I thought to be Ms. Right came back around to bite me.

Yeah, I wasn't smiling then. Having my heart broken, it was the worst thing that ever happened to me and now I'm somewhat careful who I let inside nowadays. I do understand though, that one woman does not define all women, so I'm going to try again one day, but for now a friend to share my thoughts, fears, joys and ideas with will do just fine. Yeah, by the way, as I mentioned in my last letter, I'm somewhat religious, so I do thank God for small favors, and the big ones too. Small favor, being able to express myself to a woman. The big one, well, Duh? You, of course!

Hope to hear from you at mail call. If I don't hear from you this time, I can take a hint and promise to take a hike.

And hey, take care of yourself.

Sincerely,

Eugene

Once Eugene was satisfied with his letter, he stuffed it in an envelope and dropped it in the mail. He told himself if Amanda doesn't respond, he will not make another attempt to write her. The last thing he wanted to do was burden her. Annoying her was not his goal.

Amanda decided to spend the day doing absolutely nothing but relaxing in the comfort of her home, snuggled up with one of the many goose feather pillows on her bed. She reached over for the television remote that rested on her night stand and noticed Eugene's letters sitting there. She decided to reread them. She eyed the postmarks before liberating the pages from their envelopes.

Once she refreshed her memory with his written words, she questioned herself. Should I or should I not write this guy? What would it hurt? On the one hand, he was in prison, but on the other hand, it could be fun. What am I doing anyway but sitting around the house being lazy and depressed with the world? I could use a little excitement in my life even if it was through correspondence. I will only be writing him and corresponding on my terms. I don't see any harm in that. She convinced herself to take the plunge.

She knew from her experience as an attorney that a lot of men who wind up in prison are there by circumstance or because of making a bad decision. She had known prisoners who have learned from their mistakes, got through their prison experience and in the process became all the wiser. Some even had the strength of character to go on and become wildly successful. Albeit rare, it does happen, and if Eugene desires and was motivated to better himself, then just maybe, by offering her hand in friendship, she could inspire him on his journey to succeed in life.

Deep down, in the furthest reaches of her heart and soul, Amanda hoped that one day she could find true love. She honestly believed that real love was rare, like finding a diamond buried in a mountain. But she knew that if there really was such a thing she would have to keep her mind open, look far and wide and remain hopeful. She was not a young girl anymore and she had no silly ideas about a lifelong companion just falling in her lap. She convinced herself that this may be the first step toward finding something special. Probably not, but maybe, just maybe...

Amanda rose from the bed to retrieve her laptop from the kitchen counter. She stopped at the refrigerator and poured herself a glass of Urban Mist wine, a Gila Farms signature cabernet sauvignon. She ambled back to her room and took a seat on the bed, flipped open the laptop and studied the screen for a moment before keying in the password. Her face lit up from the computer screen's glow. She carefully lifted the glass of wine to her nose, gently swirling the red liquid to better inhale the wonderful bouquet. She then slowly tilted the glass toward her lips, introducing her taste buds to the powerful flavors and aromas of red cherry and pomegranate with notes of ripe berry rounding out a lingering finish. She enjoyed the sophistication in a glass. Her spirit warmed and her fingers began to glide across the keys like a concert pianist. In a matter of minutes the letter was complete and two glasses of wine later she was satisfied with its content. Just for the sake of pure pleasure she read the letter once more before printing it out.

Chapter 9

Curtis captured my eyes with his own, probing my mind and soul of the desire that I hid deep within.

"Say baby, how about you and I go back to my place, we can talk there. We need to talk anyway, " Curtis suggested. I shook my head in negation, not trusting my own desire. I was made vulnerable by his commanding straightforwardness and deep sexy smooth voice. I didn't want to chance having my heart broken by a man who wasn't ready for an honest commitment. I knew what he wanted to talk about. We had performed these "Let's go back to my place" dates on several occasions with the same punch line. "We need to talk" being the reason for accepting his invitation. For some odd reason, we never end up talking at all. It was always straight to the bed...or stairwell...or carpet...or...

"Curtis, I can't. If you need to talk, we'll talk in public," I said, interrupting his intimate stare. If only he knew how badly I wanted him to make rhythmic beats at the parting of my hips.

He leaned closer so I could see that he was serious. "We need to talk, my place," Curtis demanded, as I made no response.

His house was only a few minutes' drive from Starbucks. The two story five bedroom, three and a half bathroom house was well appointed and spacious. Each room was furnished with a king size bed and 90-inch flat screen television. The living room area was elegantly furnished in oriental artifacts and was off limits to everyone. The den was furnished with peanut butter leather sofas positioned around a mahogany coffee table. Matching end tables were set on both sides of the sofa and a 100-inch flat screen sat at an angle in one corner. A double fireplace could be enjoyed from the living room and den. Expensive framed paintings covered the walls and the ceiling was finished with intricate African art molding and two ornate ceiling fans silently turning at low speed. Every type of game station on the market was displayed on the wall unit positioned around the high tech television.

As I walked through the home, I noticed the dining room had an antique china cabinet, a table that seats ten, decorated with fine china and Waterford crystal. The man had fine taste and took pride in his possessions. Shear opulence was captured throughout the home. My favorite part of the house was his bedroom, decorated in rich fabrics with elegant art works and antiques of African culture. The room featured a marble floor with a deep soaking tub, a huge aquarium, expensive furnishings and an oversized bed. The very room I was now being lead to by Curtis. The room was softly Litman but light could be seen at the entrance of the master bathroom. The smell of men's fragrance filled the air.

Curtis took me by surprise and kissed me deeply, then lightly shoved me to the bed. I lay back with my head propped watching him. I watched as he undressed, and gasped at the sight of his muscular chest and the way the hair ran down underneath his navel and disappeared inside his boxer briefs. The intimacy thoughts of my wanted passion made me vulnerable to the thug loving I knew was about to go down once I wrapped my arms and legs around him. I hadn't taken my eyes off the prize, biting on my bottom lip in intense excitement, as his long erection pointed directly at me. I guided him toward me. That was all it took for the real action to began. Our tongues mingled and our hands roamed each other's body freely without boundaries. The moment was treated as if it was our last.

Curtis took control as usual and introduced his lips to the right side of my lovely neck line. The warmness of his breath sent chills of enthusiasm through my soul. My moans were modest. He tenderly removed my clothing. He kissed my shoulder, my elbow, my hand, the center of my chest before taking in a nipple into his mouth. He made sure that he gave its twin equal attention before traveling south to a small volcano that was pulsating and ready to express itself through pleasurable eruption. His tongue found its target clinched the clitoris in its grasp and gently began making love to it. It throbbed within his mouth and my moans echoed a new octave. My body didn't protest the act that was being performed, my pelvis automatically thrust toward his tongue. I enjoyed the pleasures that it was giving my body. An act that I wished would never come to an end, my mind and body raced in different directions. My love muffin needed more than the intimacy of an experienced tongue, but the strength of a hard, thick, hot long stabbing sensation deep inside my soul.

Curtis knew this and he had the tool to accommodate what my love muffin was starving for. He wasted no time. The night air caressed our nudity, taking hold of his throbbing tool and escorting it between the parting of my thighs. He was invited in my tightness. The warm wetness gripped at the head. Our bodies took pride in pleasuring one another's as I knew they would, I was too far gone, I had become a slave to this man's every desire with no escape route to save my marriage in sight. Every single attribute I admired in Curtis, my husband lacked. I was torn between passion and the commitment to my marriage. Honestly, I was too weak to confront the situation.

My guilty conscious bothering me more than ever, I left Curtis's place and drove home. I arrived at my estate with every intention of patching things up with my husband. I entered my opulent home and headed down the hall toward the master bedroom. As I passed Richards office area, I noticed he was at his desk, on the phone, the door slightly ajar. I pushed the heavy oak wood door open and said, "Hello dear, I'm sorry about earlier, I..."

"Yes, that's fine, I'm busy right now, I need to reschedule an important meeting, and I'll see you later," Richard snapped, dismissing me. Evidently he was back in work mode. I knew when he was like this I would not be able to hold his attention. I would have to wait to speak with him. Feeling sullen, I retired to the bedroom.

Sitting at my vanity after a nice hot bath, I reflected on that Sunday morning in September, so many years ago, when Richard and I got engaged. I blushed at the thought, reminiscing of his smile, caring spirit, attentiveness, and loving words. I hadn't heard him speak like that in a long time. I was once madly in love with the cute boy who dared to make the lifelong commitment of marriage to me. I would have followed him across the world if that meant togetherness. I had seen the Stanford graduate reach financial success in his late twenties after investing in restaurants. International franchising, real estate and brand partnerships made him a wealthy man.

I knew my husband thrived at any business opportunity he thought could be lucrative; That was what excited him. I didn't always share in his excitement. I had not been enthusiastic about the idea of a business venture, partnering up with the legendary NBA star Magic Johnson to buy the Los Angeles Dodgers. I personally viewed that as a tragedy waiting to happen and a bad investment in a dying brand. I didn't really know if it was a bad decision or not, I came to that conclusion for no other reason than I wasn't a fan of the team, or baseball for that matter.

My conscious was at peace for not intervening in my husband's business investments because his decisions had made a fortune beyond my imagination. Before my blessing into spectacular wealth, I had imagined my future as a middle class citizen with a nice, cozy home and white picket fence.

I grew up in the affluent area around Beverly Hills, California. My father had been in construction during one of California's construction booms. He was a smart, hard driving businessman and made a fortune. The similarities between Richard and my father were obvious. The two had even become friends before my father died two years ago.

They were both wealthy men, but the thing they really had in common was how they made and watched their money. They didn't waste their money; they saved and invested wisely. I grew up with this kind of mentality so when I married Richard we were already on the same page. He would work smart and save and I would help. Our partnership was a roaring success. At fifty-one, Richard's net worth was well over seven hundred million dollars.

Ironically, my goal was never to be super rich. It just naturally worked out that way. I probably would have been happy with that middle class life and white picket fence. I wasn't complaining; it's just that my life had become dull. A gray depressing cloud began to gather in my mind. I felt guilty about thinking like this but it was the truth. I was a privileged millionaire, but bored and maybe a bit ungrateful.

It wasn't Richard's fault. I loved my husband and didn't want to throw away our life together. I knew my fling with Curtis was an attempt to spice up my life but there was something deeper, subconscious. I wasn't getting any younger and I felt that this may be my last chance to have a genuine wild romance while still young enough. It was horribly selfish. My husband was neglecting me but he didn't deserve my infidelity. I wanted to go to him and pledge my love, but Curtis had this hold on me.

That's it! The solution came to me as if it was lurking there in my mind all along. I couldn't break it off with Curtis, but maybe I didn't have to. Maybe I just needed to be with my husband. It wasn't about breaking anything off with Curtis, it was about getting back into Richard, and I knew just how to do it.

Richard was pressed for time. He had rescheduled an important business meeting. As President and CEO of Universal Services of America, Inc., the company he guided into becoming an iconic brand and a multi-million dollar business, he had enumerable responsibilities.

"Dick" Stinpindal was also a well known and influential leader in the business community. This respect allowed for him to work in various associated areas. Among his many other responsibilities, he was chairman of the International Franchising Association. Being on time for a meeting was extremely important to him.

Richard had been a stickler for professional communication, conduct and punctuality since his days at Stanford and believed his attention to this aspect of business was a big part of the reasons for his success. He refused to be late for any business meeting regardless of the situation. He believed in, "the early bird gets the worm" concept and that hard work, dedication and determination are the keys to success. As the proud owner of 216 franchises in different parts of the world, many in the enormous and lucrative emerging markets of China, he was a proven example of his ideology.

Most of his multi-unit franchises were restaurants: Kentucky Fried Chicken, MacDonald's, Pizza Hut, Subway and Jack-n-the-Box. Now he was attempting to expand into the music industry and get a piece of American Idol, and he had the perfect contact to do it.

Richard could have afforded a chauffeur but it just wasn't his style. He liked to drive fast. Breaking the speed limit from time to time was probably the only illegal thing he did. He loved those rare moments when he could jam down a southern California freeway. It reminded him of a free, innocent, fun loving time of his life; back when he was in college, when he first met MaryAnn. Those were good days and he wondered if they were gone forever.

Richard pulled his brand new BMW 750i into his parking spot in front of his company building. He was proud of this piece of real estate. He had acquired it for a song and turned the five story light industrial complex into his headquarters.

He exited the car and walked briskly to his office. He checked in with his secretary Jennifer, who said, "Your consultant is already here," pointing discreetly in the direction of the meeting. Richard made his way down the hall thinking, *Rainer was early, a man after my own heart*. When Richard entered the boardroom, only one chair was filled. It was his business development and marketing consultant.

"How are you doing sir?" Richard extended a hand.

"Mighty fine, and you?" A dapper Curtis Rainer stood and shook his hand.

Curtis and Richard had met at a business conference in New York. Richard had been so impressed with Curtis's keen knowledge during a speaking presentation, he extended an invitation to partner up with him.

Richard wanted into the music and entertainment industry and he saw Curtis as his conduit to success.

They have been business partners for a few years now. Curtis had assisted him with several advertising campaigns for his restaurants. They worked well together, persuading media executives and associated business professionals to see their vision. They both perfected the art of negotiation by combining their authentic nature with their eye for strategy in the boardroom. Curtis was a pure genius when it came to marketing. He just had that gift. Plus he was knowledgeable and respected in the music and entertainment field. If he said things were a certain way, then that's the way it was.

A short while after they began their conversation, Richard began to appear preoccupied, "Are you all right?" Curtis asked.

"Everything is fine," Richard said, attempting to shake Curtis's interest. But Curtis was an expert at deciphering what was really behind a look or comment, and Richard knew this. Attempting to hide the truth was no use. Curtis already knew there was something bugging him.

"It's the wife, I need to spend more time...I've been neglecting her."

"Oh yeah?" Curtis said inquisitively.

"We've been married so long now, it's..." Richard searched for the right words, "You know how they get," Richard said.

"Yeah, they sure get funny when you don't give them enough attention," Curtis said.

"I got a way to fix it," Richard offered objectively, in a way that makes the marital issue sound like a business challenge he was working to overcome.

Curtis wisely read the look in Richard's eye and said,

"You're not going to take her to dinner and a movie, are you?"

"Why not?" Richard inquired defensively. Then, more thoughtfully, "Damn, I'm so busy and out of touch these days. I have a beautiful wife, I have everything. I love her, everything about her." He stared at a picture of his wife on the screen of his iPhone, leaned over and showed Curtis.

The black man went pale. Curtis was stunned. He couldn't believe his eyes. It was MaryAnn.

Curtis gave Richard some advice. "Be spontaneous, different. Think about things she might like to do that you know she had never done, and do it. It'll feel new, fresh, you know what I mean?" He only hopes Richard hadn't noticed his surprise at seeing the iPhone image.

"Like bondage? S and M?" Richard said excitedly.

"What?" Curtis said, surprised that Richard went there so quickly. Curtis continued, "What the hell are you talking about? I didn't say anything like that." Chuckling about how crazy Richard sounded. "Man what the hell is wrong with you?"

"Oh, I thought that's what you were talking about," Richard said sheepishly.

"No, that's not what I was talking about, but if you think that might do the trick, then whatever floats your boat." Curtis said, wondering if his memories of he and MaryAnn on their escapade to the Bahamas were affecting his judgment now.

Chapter 10

The "Legal Environment of Business" college textbook wasn't as intimidating as the Chinese mandarin language course Eugene had been studying for the past seven weeks, but challenging nonetheless. Summer semester final exams were in three days and Eugene felt unprepared and overwhelmed at the very thought of being tested on the material. With little support from other students or a professor, correspondence courses in prison could be difficult. It was just the inmate, his textbook, and how much effort he was willing to put into his studies.

Eugene questioned himself why he had taken the classes, knowing that summer semester was only eight weeks long, unlike the usual sixteen week fall and spring semesters. He knew there was no sense in crying over spilled milk, what's done was done. He would have to cram and study as much as he could within the shortened time frame. That meant he would have to abandon several of his other activities and projects he was involved with.

Eugene aimlessly eyed the textbooks before becoming restless at the very challenge of tackling the pages. He reached over and turned the knob on his clear plastic eight inch oscillating fan. The plastic blades propelled at a low speed. The cool breeze introduced itself to the right side of his face but the airflow was not the reason for turning the fan on. It was the serenity and relaxation he found in the humming sound it made.

He forced his eyes to indulge a few pages of the thick textbook before losing interest in studying. He had a better idea.

He rumbled through his locker and removed a stack of unlined white paper and set it on the painted metal surface of the empty top bunk. He then removed a black leather eye glass case from the inside door of the locker and liberated one of the dozens of ink pens it contained.

Restlessly he began writing a scene to his new novel, "The Green Rose." After completing a single paragraph, his writing objective was over. Boredom mixed with exhaustion kicked in. He hadn't slept well in a week and it was evident in his lack of creativity. All he wanted to do was lay down on his bunk and rest.

As he began to unfold the white cotton blanket, the loud clang of heavy keys echoed in the hall. The telltale sound meant that a correctional officer was on his way down the concrete corridor. The officer abruptly clanged the oversized brass key into the keyhole and manually unlocked the heavy steel door to cell twenty-two. Eugene rose to his feet quickly to investigate the officer's intentions. Sometimes corrections officers will rush a cell in an attempt to find contraband, cuff-up an inmate to investigate some perceived prison rules violation or conduct a routine cell search. However, the reason for this unlock became quickly apparent. Officer Hernandez stood at the cell entrance with a hand full of letters.

"Mail call, gentlemen," he announced, carefully eyeing the mail over his handlebar moustache as he flipped through the stack, "When I call your name give me your last two...Banuelos."

"Seven zero," came a reply from somewhere within the cell, Felipe recited the last two numbers of his inmate ID number but didn't move to retrieve his mail.

"Pena," the officer announced, separating the letters from the stack. Jerry Pena rose from his bunk where he was drawing and ambled forward toward the cell door.

"Lewis."

"Five eight," Colton responded but didn't attempt to move. He remained lying propped up on his bunk reading a huge textbook titled "Abnormal Psychology."

"Weems."

"Six three," Eugene followed suit.

The officer handed off all the mail to Jerry before securing the lock on the wide steel door and venturing on to his next destination.

Following one of the many informal procedures the men had worked out for themselves in the four double bunk cell, Jerry carefully distributed the mail. He placed Eugene's letter on top of the empty bunk Eugene used as a writing surface.

Eugene picks up the letter and casually glances at the name and return address. Not immediately recognizing the name, he reads it again. His spirit soars as he realizes who the letter was from, Amanda Aniston. Tenderly he opens the envelop, as if handling a precious item. He slides the letter from its thin paper shell. He hoped there might be a picture inside, but there was no pearl in this oyster. He would have to be satisfied with Amanda's written words.

Greetings, Mr. Weems,

How are you, Sir? I hope this missive reaches you in good spirits and wonderful health.

I received your letters. Unfortunately, I am extra guarded and very dubious about corresponding with a prisoner. That was why I hadn't replied to your letters until now. I'm sure you can understand my position. I was intrigued with how well you express yourself, so I decided, Why not? I'll give this pen pal thing a try.

As you know, my name is Amanda. I'm forty-eight years young, divorced, and Caucasian. I have long blond hair and big blue eyes. I am of medium build, well proportioned and am told very attractive. You mention that you had the pleasure of seeing a photo of me, so I'll allow you to be the judge. However, my beauty was not where I would like to focus at this moment.

I am open to establishing a friendship with someone that I can express my inner thoughts and emotions with, who will not judge me, who will instead be a good listener. I would like to offer the same in return. I am not looking for a boyfriend or husband, simply a pen friend. I want to get to know someone for exactly who they are. I have been in one long-term relationship that ended in divorce, leaving much damage in its wake and many emotional scars. I'm not quick to trust anyone. If you ever gain my complete trust and are welcomed into my world, consider it an honor, not to be taken for granted. I'm a God fearing woman one hundred percent, and will accept nothing less than a God fearing man. I'm very well educated with three college degrees. My major was criminal justice. I've enjoyed studying law ever since I was a kid. I can answer some legal questions, but I'm no longer a lawyer and laws vary from state to state, changing all the time. I was a lawyer in New York for awhile, but now I run a successful corporation. I have no kids. Things I enjoy are traveling the world, shopping, and being pampered with facials, manicures and pedicures. And I'm always up for girls night out with my close friends. I am outgoing in public, but subdued in my private life. I can count on one hand the people I would consider my closest friends. I spoil myself rotten. I want what I want, when I want it, how I want it, and from whom I want it. Not being snobbish, just being honest.

Okay, now let's get a couple things out in the open before moving on with this journey of communication we are attempting to establish with one another. I will not be your financial provider. I have a good idea what it's like in there. I don't miss an episode of "Orange was the New Black." You must get your honey buns and stamps how you live.

So how long are you in for? How much time have you served? I only asked out of curiosity. Are you going to church in there? that's important, you know. My concern was that many people find God in prison, but forget about Him when they get out. Sometimes God breaks people down in order to build them up again. God will get your attention in many ways. So before I give you my number, I'd like to correspond for awhile. I hope that's okay with you. I'm sure you understand.

I look forward to hearing from you. Take care and keep God first.

Sincerely,

Amanda

It was four in the afternoon. In the California State prison system, four o'clock meant it was standing count time. All inmates had to be at their assigned bunks. "Count," as inmates and staff referred to it, was the only time corrections officers walked through the housing units, or blocks, and methodically counted every prisoner.

Around this time, cell 22 was usually quiet. The guys were often reading letters they had received, writing response letters, quietly studying or napping. Since letter writing was cheaper than long distance phone calls and could be thoughtfully done in the cell, it was a common practice. Although they were living in the digital information age and in one of the most technologically advanced societies in the world, in California, nearly every prisoner hand wrote, sent and received paper letters.

After lying back on his bunk and reading Amanda's

letter, Eugene sat up, passed the letter to Colton and said, "You ever heard of a tee-vee show called "The New Orange was Black"?

"Yeah," Colton said, dropping the open book to his chest and taking the letter. "I think it's some kind of prison show or something. I've never seen it, though."

"Yeah, that's what it sounds like," Eugene said, then, pointing to the letter already in Colton's hand, "read that, tell me what you think."

Eugene rarely shared a letter with other inmates, but he respected Colton's opinion and a letter from a new girl was important. He wanted to hear what Colton thought about Amanda.

Colton was happy to oblige. He knew Eugene wouldn't interrupt his study time for something frivolous. Colton began reading the letter as Eugene gets up and starts to prepare a meal.

Prisoners have a canteen and can buy items to cook for themselves. Using dehydrated beans, rice, squeeze cheese, mayonnaise, sausage, cans of chili, shredded beef, tortillas, nachos and an assortment of spices and some creativity, one could make a halfway decent meal.

Eugene filled a hot-pot with water and plugs it in, balancing the electric water heating device on the sink so the faucet can still be used.

Eugene was a master prison chef and in fact had been lead cook at another prison. He was noted for his culinary skills and routinely cooked custom meals for prison staff. The meals he managed to create in the cell were excellent.

Colton had tried in-cell cooking once. One of their previous cellies had tried one of Colton's burritos, promptly made a face and said, "Man, this is horrible." As this particular inmate had been seen eating from prison trash cans, it was a brutal comment and it initiated a chorus of criticism. Much to everyone's relief, Colton never cooked again. Eugene cooked, Colton did the dishes. That was the arrangement everyone preferred. They shared costs and the stash was stored in Colton's locker and under his bunk.

Eugene was six-two and had been a professional athlete back in the day. His fighting weight was two hundred and fifteen pounds. At forty, and with plenty of his own excellent cooking, he was now soaring north of two-fifty.

As Eugene opened the thin metal door and rummaged through Colton's locker for ingredients, he reminded Colton of a camping trip Colton's family had taken when he was a kid. Must have been in Yellowstone or up in Canada somewhere, as he recalled. In the middle of the night there had been a ruckus, and in the morning Colton's father found the cause of the commotion. A grizzly bear had ripped the door off the trunk of the neighboring camper's car. He was after an igloo cooler full of sweet grape juice within. The episode was evidenced by the teeth marks on the lid of the juice cooler.

As Colton reminisced, Eugene mumbled something into the locker. Colton couldn't help but chuckle out loud. Eugene even sounded a little bit like that grizzly.

"Huh?" Eugene asks, assuming Colton had found something funny about the letter.

Not wishing to share his childhood memories at that moment and wanting to rib his friend about the letter, Colton said, "Oh, she said you got to get your honey buns and stamps how you live. I was thinking about telling you the same thing, Smart lady."

Colton resisted the temptation to look for bite marks on the locker and realized where the cookies he had put in there must have disappeared to.

"Yeah, you see that?" Eugene asks.

Both men smile now. The idea that a sophisticated

woman on the streets knew all about prison life because of a television show she watched was...cute.

Colton knew that Eugene had no intention of asking this girl for money. He wasn't that kind of guy. He worked for his. But in truth, there were a lot of prisoners who wrote women to try and get money from them. Colton thought her mention of this practice in her first letter to Eugene was funny, but wise.

"Guess she ain't gonna put up with you hittin' her up for a book of stamps," Colton said, knowing how ridiculous that sounded.

"Yeah, I already like her," Eugene responds.

"You going to write her back?" asks Colton.

"What you think?" Eugene said, stopping his cooking long enough to give Colton an incredulous look. "Hell, yeah, I'm going to write her back. I'm going to write her back as soon as I'm done eatin', you can bet your last dollar on that."

The meal, joined by Jerry and Felipe, was delicious. Colton broke out his Ajax soap and sponge and did his part, Felipe and Jerry pitched in. Eugene washed and dried his hands and began composing a letter to Amanda. It didn't take him long in doing so. As usual, he reread the letter before mailing it out to Amanda.

SHOOTER: Eugene Weems T-40463
                P.O. Box 92
                Chowchilla, CA 93610
TARGET: Amanda Aniston
AIM: Your mind, heart, soul and hand in
                Friendship

Hello Amanda,

It was another pleasant day in my life today. I felt the need to share that with you, partly because you were the reason for it. Yes, a letter received for a letter sent was always a good thing in my predicament. I guess I don't have to tell you, which was even better.

A surprise it was to read that bit of personal information about you. I would have never imagined. I guess it's true what they say about good things coming out of some of the most unexpected places. Diamonds from coal, pearls from oysters, etcetera. But you, I'm just surprised is all. I'm smiling on the inside, because I'm convinced that you might be able to understand me. That is so hard for so many people to do. Not that I'm complicated, just not meant for anyone to read me.

Unique as I may be, I think I might have found more than just a cage in common with you.

Like for instance, our passion for literacy and getting ahead in life, achieving goals. I can honestly say without a doubt that I'm on a mission to obtain and enjoy the finer things in life, to experience new ventures as I travel down the road of success. And I hope on this narrow passage of opportunity that faith had our paths crossing. I hope this invitation into one another's world will be the window that shows us that true friendship was possible, and trust, love, and loyalty can be a beautiful thing when it's been built on a solid foundation. Have you ever trusted and loved someone to the point that loyalty was not a question? Isn't that a wonderful feeling?

I thank you for writing me back. It means a great deal to me to know that there are people that still exist in society who have compassion for a lost soul, of which I am one.

I look forward to the time we'll spend conversing on many topics, I'm sure. Feel free to asked me any questions your heart desires. I'm sure you have many. It's been a pleasure reading your words and having the attention of a lady. I await the next opportunity to be given the pleasure of acquainting myself with you even further.

With that said, I close with this poem.

Thank you for being a beautiful rose and my friend.

Thank you for giving me the opportunity to inhale your essence that inspired my heart to take the chance to love again.

If this was a game for me to win your heart,

Best believe I am in it to win it.

And as you can see, it's hard on a brotha' when you're in a place of incarceration, but what makes it a little bit easier was when you have a beautiful rose as a friend to share your personal feelings with.

So, my beautiful rose, I hope at the end of this poem you will see that I am grateful just to have my words in your presence, and the offer of your hand in friendship.

So today I thank Santa Clause for the early Christmas gift

And Cupid for the love arrow that was connecting our hearts.

Thank you for you.

Sincerely,

Your friend, Eugene

Two months quickly flew by and Amanda and Eugene were still going strong with their correspondence. She looked forward to receiving the ten-page letters he was writing to her daily. She decided that he was the best thing that had happened to her since her divorce. Eugene made her smile with his humor and with all the attention he was giving her, she felt special, needed and loved. Girl's night out with Kathryn and MaryAnn had become the center stage for conversation about Eugene and his life behind prison walls.

The women were intrigued with the stories Amanda

shared about her incarcerated friend and how sweet and attentive he was. They noticed changes in her. She was no longer depressed and distant. She was now glowing, happy as-all-can-be, with a vibrant, spirited pep in her step. At times, her new attitude caused her to be misunderstood. It appeared as if she was a lady with a swagger. Some women were envious, but her friends were happy for her.

Several even wanted to experience this newfound happiness Amanda had, but commitment to their marriages kept them at bay, compelling them to live their fantasies vicariously through Amanda's experiences. MaryAnn was excited for her friend, but a little baffled at how their roles had changed. Now, she was the one who was depressed. She had a husband who wasn't interested in her and she honestly missed Curtis.

Amanda decided it was time to hear the voice of the man she had been acquainting herself with. She decided at that moment to send Eugene her phone number.

Eugene received a letter from Amanda with the words "CALL ME" written in bold letters across the entire page. He folded the letter and secured it in his front shirt pocket and headed straight for the phones. He hadn't signed up for a phone call, but he wasn't about to let that impede him from calling Amanda. He waited impatiently for one of the four day room phones to become available. When one did, he raced toward it, removing the receiver, tucking it between his shoulder and neck. He then removed the letter from his shirt pocket and unfolded it. He studied the number before keying in the digits.

The phone rang and the anticipation made him nervous when she picked up. The recording system came on; an automated message repeatedly interrupts any call made from prison. An anonymous digital voice makes clear that the call originates from within the California state prison system.

The collect call was accepted and there was a moment of silence on both ends before Eugene decided to take the lead.

"Hello," Eugene's baritone voice breaks the silence, serenading the airwaves.

"Hi Eugene, what a pleasure," Amanda sounded excited.

"No, the pleasure is all mine," he shot back.

"Your voice was not what I imagined it would sound like."

"Oh! I don't know if that's a good thing or not. What did you imagine it would sound like?" Eugene asked.

"I don't know, but I didn't think it would be so deep, smooth and sexy," Amanda confessed.

"Hmmm...sorry to disappoint you," Eugene joked.

"No disappointment here. So, how much longer do you have to go?"

"About three more years, just enough time for us to fall in love, get married, have lots of conjugal visits and live happily ever after. Just kidding, unless that's really something you see us doing. It's all good."

"Marriage...really...honey, I don't think so, never again, but then I am a hopeless romantic and I do believe in never-say-never. Marrying to have sex..." she laughs out loud. "That would be interesting, and the story of my life," Amanda played along.

"Yeah, it could be the story of our lives. You know what, Amanda, I really like your style, your spirit. You're a remarkable woman. You make me feel like my old self again."

"What do you mean by that?" she asked.

"What I mean is, I can see myself with you. I need a relationship that matters to me. I need to have someone close to me that I am willing to succeed for. I need a woman in my life, someone I could put before myself. I know that it might sound awkward for someone you just met to mention marriage and conjugal visits, but it is something that would be considered anyway. I have never been married and never had any children. In one of my letters I sent to you, I believe I mentioned that I am a professional kick boxer and well traveled. I didn't have time to slow down to plant seeds. I am grateful that I did not have any children. I would have left them in a bad situation. They would be without a father there to protect them. But maybe when I get out..." Eugene spoke from the heart. He truly believed honesty was the best policy when establishing a sustainable relationship up front and in the beginning. He was enjoying the conversation with Amanda, even though he was doing most of the talking.

"Wow, mister, you have left a girl with a lot to think about. I didn't foresee all of this coming my way," Amanda admits.

"Babe, please forgive me if I've come off a little too strong. I don't mean to overwhelm you or scare you off. I'm just expressing myself to you. I'm sure you can appreciate that. I've been without the touch of a woman for over fourteen years. Can you imagine my desires? Just to hear your sweet voice takes my imagination on a journey of its own. What good is a man without a woman? Without you, a man can't truly live life, so babe, show me your strong side. Don't be scared to step into something new. I will always cherish and lift you up like you deserve. Don't let what you think others will think about you, deter you. Be a leader and do this with me, babe. I will cherish you, or you could wait for a lying ass cheater, excuse my French," he pauses before continuing. "So many options in society can lead to meeting someone who will lie to you and hurt you again.

Not me, though. I'm here, and with all this love to shower over you."

"Eugene, it sounds so enticing and you seem so sincere and sweet, but we don't know each other, we just recently met. I have yet to meet you in person. conjugal visits sound really nice and fun, but we can't, I couldn't. Who does that? I can't, I'm sorry, Eugene."

"Yeah, I'm sorry too. It was too bad we can't get around committing to being husband and wife in order to have conjugal visits. I say too bad, because it sounds like marriage was not in your view of the near future. But shootin' straight and keepin' true to my desire for a good woman, I have to admit that I wouldn't want it no other way. Makin' love, enjoying the taste of your flesh, and sharing the most pleasurable intimacies of your essence, would only make sense if you were my wife. I would not even want to see you in any other light than that of the Queen you are. Baby, bottom line though, there ain't no way around getting' those conjugal visits without sayin' 'I do.' Say it, babe, don't be scared. I won't hurt you. Plus, if I don't get this off my chest right now, my heart is going to pop. So here goes. Amanda, come up here and give me some of you. Let's get a room for three days and two nights. We'll talk and work it all out with fruit and honey on top, of you, that is. Will you be my lady? Can I have you to claim as my own? Worst case scenario, you say no, we'll still be friends. So what do I got to lose? Spoil me now with all your love and affection, and my next proposal might find us getting conjugal visits, eating good food, cuddling and watching movies," Eugene expressed.

Amanda found herself listening more than anything. For a moment, she thought the conversation she was having with Eugene was a dream, and wanted to remain asleep to see how it played out. But then the recording came on, announcing that they had sixty seconds left before the call ended. Amanda was not ready for her Knight in Shining Armor's soothing voice to stop serenading her innermost, deepest desires. So she blurted out, "Can you please call me right back?"

There was a possibility that he could if he chose to take the risk of being busted and suffering the consequences for breaking institutional rules.

"Sure can. I'll call you back right now," Eugene quietly agreed to do so, disregarding the fact that he may be taking another inmate's assigned phone time. Eugene couldn't care less if he was busted or not, his only concern was calling Amanda back as he said he would.

He was craving this woman's attention and had so much to say in such a small amount of time. As soon as he had a dial tone, he redialed the number. This time, she answered the phone right away, and went through the normal formalities to accept the collect call.

She was like a child in a candy store, enjoying the sweetness of Eugene words, it was everything that she needed to hear to validate herself as a desirable woman. His expressions were so heartfelt and sincere, for the first time in a long time she felt needed, admired, loved and happy. If Eugene was a fairy tale prince, then this would be one story she didn't want to come to an end. Eugene made her feel like she was in high school again with a sweetheart crush. They both enjoyed each other's company. They spoke as if they had known each other their entire life, flirting with one another and playing the "What if" game.

Three phone calls later, Amanda asked Eugene if she could come visit him. Eugene was open to visitations. He liked that idea. He needed a change of scenery from his daily life behind prison walls. To be able to hold the hands and smell the scent of a woman was a gift in itself. The thought of getting a warm hug or being able to sit down across from a woman and have lunch was a huge deal to him.

He explained to Amanda the process she would need to complete in order to get approved to visit him. He described the visiting form and assured her he would send one in the mail as soon as he gets off the phone. The phone call ended too soon.

It would take a while for Amanda to get approved, but Eugene returned to his cell excited anyway. For him, a few weeks would pass in a minute. He was just happy she wanted to visit and he looked forward to seeing her.

Chapter 11

Curtis returned from his meeting with Richard knowing what he had to do. His relationship with MaryAnn had run its course. His only hope now was that everything would work out for the best.

Curtis had a way with women for as long as he could remember. This thing with MaryAnn wasn't anything new to him, although she was his first white girl. He did like her, she was cool and a lot more laid back and real than he had imagined a privileged white woman would be. He most definitely had enjoyed his time with her.

He needed to see her again. He picked up his phone and tapped her icon.

"Hello," MaryAnn answered on the first ring.

"Hey lil' momma, it's me. What are you doin?"

"Oh, hi. I was just speaking with Richard. He was telling me about one of his partners in the baseball team thing," she said.

"The Dodgers?" Curtis clarifies.

"Yeah," she said, and added in a surge of loyalty to her husband of over twenty-five years, "He really is brilliant."

"I'm sure he is," Curtis said. "look, I want to see you tonight. How about my place, eight o'clock?"

"I don't know, Curtis, I'm kind of tired," she was

desperately trying to find a way out of seeing Curtis again.

"This is important; I really need to see you." There was urgency in his voice. This surprised MaryAnn a little bit and she was intrigued. Why does he need to see her so bad?

"Okay, I'll be there," she caved in.

"See you then," he confirmed before ending the call.

I arrived at Curtis's place and rang the bell on the front door. In my heart I did not want to stay the night, but my heart wasn't the part of my body that was controlling me these days.

Curtis answered the door dressed in a finely tailored business suit. Strangely, there was no music playing, no wine in sight, and there was a two-piece Luis Vuitton luggage set packed and placed by the front door in preparation for a trip. It was as if Curtis was getting ready to go somewhere.

"Hi, MaryAnn," Curtis said as he hugged me. "I'm glad you could make it."

"Are you going somewhere? Looks like your bags are packed," I gestured toward the luggage.

"I'm flying to New York tonight, ten o'clock. I signed a new R&B artist. He's fresh, smooth and real cool, but a bit green," Curtis smiled at the thought of his new prospect. "I'll need to develop him. We are going into the studio, so I'll be back east for awhile."

"Oh, I thought it might be another one of our nights," I feigned disappointment.

"But you didn't bring your overnight bag," Curtis pointed out.

"Curtis..." I began.

"MaryAnn," he interrupted me. "Who are we kidding? We had a wonderful time. We did our thing, but it's time to move on."

I couldn't believe it. He was breaking it off with me! Stunned, all I could do was listen.

"I've been getting around for a minute, and I've learned a few things. You are special, MaryAnn, a truly unique, beautiful and exotic flower. Unfortunately, we are not meant to be together. It just isn't right, don't you agree?" he asked, sensing my relief.

"You could be right." I hugged my lover, perhaps for the last time. A teardrop rolled down my cheek, but the tear was not for Curtis. I wept for Richard, a tear of relief and love for him. At that moment, I realized the affair may have reinvigorated my feelings for my husband.

"Okay, lil momma," Curtis said tenderly, pulling himself away from me, noticing the tears but sensing they were not for him. "I'm goin' now." He grabbed my hand and I walked with him out the door and to his car. I let go of his hand as he dropped into the seat.

"Good-bye, Curtis," I gave him a dim smile.

He closed the car door, the engine fired to life, and he drove off into the night.

A page in a chapter of my life had been turned. I would forever remember Curtis, but it was over.

Richard decided to take a detour from his original plan as he pulled up in front of an exclusive country club and allowed an eager valet to take his keys. He stepped out of his car and walked a cobble stone path cutting through a finely landscaped area around a classic southern Californian red tiled roof and stucco building to enter through a side double door. The high-end country club maintained a small but fully functional winery. He loved the scent of the aging wine soaked oaken barrels lined up within. The club's winery always reminded him of class and the importance of time. *You just can't rush quality* he thought as he walked through the small house and tasting areas.

He continued through the interior of the club, passing a cigar and fine tobacco shop on his way over to the auxiliary bar. Richard wanted to avoid the main restaurant and lounge areas. He preferred the quiet, more private, smoke shop bar. He entered the lush but dimly lighted establishment remembering the respected business associate who brought him here years ago. They had closed a huge deal making them millions and felt entitled to some high quality, personal entertainment. This secluded area of the club was frequented by the kinds of people who could accommodate every type of desire.

He knew from past experience that his favorite hangout spot attracted some of the most exotic females in the entertainment business. He wanted to make sure he had a full view of the trophy pieces who lurked in the shadows looking to have a good time. He wanted to make sure he had the drop on the prize.

"Well, well, look what boredom has dragged in. You must be cunt hunting." Diane Smith exclaimed, with a devilish grin revealing sparklingly, even, white teeth from behind the bar. Diane was a black Marilyn Monroe lookalike who maintained an air of a woman accustomed to a privileged lifestyle.

Richard looked her up and down, admiring her honey roasted smooth complexion and dyed blond curls draping her delicate golden shoulders. Her lush breasts seemed to be staring at him, and struggling for a way out of the red crop scoop tank top that displayed her curvaceous, slender midriff adorned with a glinting diamond navel ring. She stood wide legged in a pair of stretch white fitted jeans outlining her thick hips and thighs.

"Richard honey," she stated as Richard gazed up into her penetrating hazel blues that sparkled like two polished sapphires. "I heard you and your wife are having marital problems," she paused to probe his face before continuing. "See now darlin', you can't keep spending all your free time up in places like this. A woman requires some quality time." If only she had known her words were on the money. Richard, however was not about to confirm her speculation. "Like I've told you many times before, I'll say it again, you need to start spending more time at home, instead of at the office and here at this damn bar."

"Good to see you too, Diane," Richard said sarcastically, ignoring her advice. "I never knew you cared so much about my marriage and happiness, but it's good to know that I have a secret admirer who cares about me from a distance. You should stop playing hard to get and come home with me so I wouldn't have to go through these lectures you enjoy subjecting me to."

Diane leaned onto the bar to gaze closely at him, attempting to discern if he was serious. Interrupting his intimate stare, she smiled at his flirtatious words. "Yeah, you must be insane or a sick one," she placed the back of her hand against his forehead thinking that he may be coming down with a fever. "In your dreams honey," she added removing her hand before ambling off. Richard watched her body sway gracefully as if she was keeping up with a rhythmic beat that no one heard but herself. Her hips appeared to move independently but in concert with the rest of her as she walked down to the other end of the bar to wait on a customer.

Damn, now that's what I need in my bed to jazz up my marriage, he thought. The idea of bringing another woman into the bedroom with his wife was appealing to him, although he wasn't sure what the wife might think about it. This was just one of the many ideas to fix his marriage that had crossed his mind.

Richard actually enjoyed Diane's disciplinary attitude

toward him. Being dominated by the opposite sex turned him on, making him wonder what it would've been like to have Diane as his wife. He always had fantasies of being with an African American woman. It was a fantasy he dared not explore until now. Its true what they say, necessity was the mother of invention. The discussion he had with Curtis had opened a Pandora's box and his imagination was now getting away from him. He found himself constantly plotting his marriage saving debut.

Amanda noticed that MaryAnn had developed an attitude toward Eugene. Now, for some reason, she was against the idea of Amanda corresponding with a prisoner. She had turned into a real snobbish negative bitch to say the least, Amanda thought. MaryAnn had become pessimistic about everything now that her lover had flown back east never to return to her arms. It was obvious she was unhappy and became irritable at the mention of Eugene's name.

Amanda quickly picked up on what was transpiring between her and MaryAnn. So she came to the conclusion to keep her personal life to herself and not mention the visiting form she had received from Eugene. Amanda removed the letter from her purse, read it and then carefully examined the visiting questionnaire. *Wow! They want to know your life history,* she said to no one, removing a pen from a side pocket on her purse. Once it was filled out she stuffed it in an envelope, rose from the bar and left. There were no goodbyes, see you later or take care...absolutely nothing. She refused to let MaryAnn rob her of the piece of happiness she felt with Eugene. She was the very person who introduced them and now she was trying to tear them apart. Amanda wasn't going for it and she wasn't going to sit around and listen to no one speak negative about Eugene, not even her best friend. Girls night out was over before it had begun.

Eugene was kicking back on his bunk with his new touch screen tablet. The California Department of Corrections and Rehabilitation was struggling with bringing the antiquated, backwards, and sometimes brutal California state prison system into the modern era. But as Eugene was scrolling through the UTAB-7's detailed digital dictionary, he thought. Valley State Prison, under Warden Ron Davis, was heading in the right direction.

Eugene had been down fourteen years and had never used anything like this thing. As he tapped and navigated his way through this wonderful little device, Jerry handed him a folded and stapled piece of white paper and his day was brightened even more. It was the visitor approval notice for Amanda. He carefully set the Tablet down and tore the staple from the folded paper. He was stoked when he read the words, "The person indentified above has requested approval to visit with you. His/Her request had been approved. It is your responsibility to inform your visitor." Amanda was cleared to visit, life was good.

"Hell yeah, baby was approved." Excitement over took his emotions. Tears of joy gathered at the corners of his eyes. A sense of hope replenished his spirit. His lungs seemed to take a fresh breath, signaling a new start in life that wasn't polluted with the surrounding air of condemnation.

He hurried out of the cell to the day room, scoped out the scenery before zeroing in on an unoccupied phone booth. Inmates who beckoned for his attention were shunned. Many inmates looked up to Eugene and were quick to bring him their complaints about prison life. He had no patience for entertaining the concerns of these constant whiners about their living conditions, or anything else. Not at the moment anyways.

He was on a mission with one goal in mind, and that mission was to secure a phone call. He needed to call Amanda to inform her she could visit. Over his years of incarceration he had become adept at getting on the heavily crowded prison phone. Without hesitation he gracefully claimed the booth and began entering Amanda's digits. Amanda must have been anticipating his call because she picked up on the first ring. She went through the formalities required for accepting the call and said,

"Hello there, Mr. Weems."

"Hello to you too, gorgeous," Eugene responded.

"You must have been reading my mind, I was just thinking about you before you called," Amanda confessed. Eugene was all teeth. He liked the idea of having someone who cared enough to think of him. It felt good, he felt loved.

"Guess what?" He asked avoiding the specific question on purpose.

"How 'bout I don't, and you just tell me," She replied sweetly.

"You been approved to visit," He couldn't wait to tell her.

"What? Really? You're not pulling my leg are you?" Amanda said excitedly.

"Naw babe, you been approved, I'm holdin' the paper in my hand right now." he assured her, fanning the paper as if she could read it. Amanda went silent.

When she learned her visiting application had been approved, she immediately logged onto the Visitor Processing Appointment Scheduling System (VPASS) website and scheduled an appointment for the following weekend to visit Eugene. She wanted to do everything in her power to expedite the visitation process. Eugene had provided her with the web address a few weeks prior so she could familiarize herself with the visitation process and rules of the institution.

"Hello?" Eugene said into the receiver.

"Sorry dear, I'm still here," Amanda said

"I was just checking cause you got quiet on me," Eugene said.

"Oh, I was doing something on the laptop," she purposely avoided telling Eugene that she had made an appointment to see him. Her mind was now wondering about what she was going to wear when she visited. She had many outfits that she looked cute in but she needed to make sure she was in compliance with the visitor dress code for the Valley State Prison visit room. Eugene noticed that Amanda was distracted with something so he decided to make up an excuse why he had to get off the phone. He didn't like to think that he was interrupting something.

"Babe, I have to run, I got to handle a few things. I'll talk to you later." He ended the call before she could get a word in.

Chapter 12

Last year, over breakfast, Richard had insisted that I read a magazine article. While Men's Journal magazine was not my normal reading material, I did enjoy the article. As I recalled, it was about fly fishing in Patagonia. Evidently, according to this adventure magazine, there were cabins along glorious mountain streams and rivers where abundant fish and game thrived. The author of the article wrote as if he was describing El Dorado. With streams full of golden, Chilean trout that jumped on the hook, sweeping vistas from the porch of well appointed mountain cabins and sunsets as beautiful in all the world.

Richard kept going on and on about it for weeks. He said he never realized there was trout fishing in the Andes and how he loved to fish streams in the Sierra with his father when he was a kid. He went on and on about how unspoiled and wonderful it must be down there. He said, "If I was going to get away, that's where I would go." He even attempted to plan a trip and bought tickets. But business plans always trumped and he was forced to cancel.

I knew that was the place I could take him. I began researching flights to Buenos Aires, Argentina and Santiago, Chili. I looked into everything from helicopter flights to secluded fishing cabins to llama caravans. I would plan things out so Richard could not refuse, I would surprise him. I chartered a flight. I knew my husband. Once he was there he would want to stay for a while. I would make sure of that. After all, I was a woman. I knew what I possessed between my thighs was the antidote to my problem. Provide the husband some quality time to play with the kitty cat and his nose would be wide open to my every beck and call. The plan to reunite our marriage was mapped out. All the pieces to pull it off were now in play. I just hoped that my body wouldn't reject my husband's intimate touch after being caressed and pleasured by a well endowed gentleman of the streets, the man I constantly thought of, Curtis.

I contemplated calling Amanda to say hello and to inform her that I would be out of town for a while, but I decided against it. I was still appalled at how she up and left during girl's night out. Several days had passed since then and Amanda hadn't attempted to contact me. That was unlike her. *If Amanda was going to choose Eugene over me, so be it. She'll come running back when he breaks her heart*, I told myself, wishing the worst for my friend.

Saturday morning had arrived. Amanda was up bright and early preparing for her trip to the prison. She browsed through her large collections of gowns, choosing a mermaid cut versus an A-line. She loved how the mermaid cut gowns accentuated her hips and waist. It was important to her that she made a red carpet grand entrance to light up Eugene's smile.

She added the finishing touches to her beauty before slipping her feet into a pair of gold stilettos. She modeled the dress in front of a full size mirror. *Stunning,* she said before reaching for her handbag and ambling out of the hotel. The limousine she had requested was waiting for her. She had planned going in style.

It only took the limousine twenty minutes to drive from Fresno out to the prison in Chowchilla. Amanda had been nervous, not knowing what to expect. She had perceived the prison to be like those old prisons she had seen in the movies, dark, foreboding, surrounded by barking dogs, electric fences and razor wire. To her surprise, upon arriving in the parking lot of where a prison was supposed to be, she found a quiet facility recessed within a well manicured landscape. To a casual observer Valley State Prison could be easily confused with a community college or university. This place, she thought, was every bit a modern institution.

The sight eased her nervousness. The luxurious car stopped in front of the visiting building entrance. The chauffer stepped out and rushed around the vehicle to get the door. Amanda got out of the car as if expecting a paparazzi assault. She smiled, turning her head here and there for imaginary photographers waiting to take her picture as she walked down a pretend red carpet.

Amanda went through the institution's check-in process and was directed to the visiting area. She entered the visiting room and heads turned as if she had been nominated for an Oscar. Correctional officers scrambled to assist her, attempting to recall her celebrity status, wondering who she was. They escorted her to the visiting room so she could check in with the officer seated behind the podium.

Veteran Correctional Officer Barnett was working overtime today, and the visit room was not his ordinary assignment, but he immediately noticed Amanda as she entered and approached the podium. *Wow, this lady has class*, he thought. "Good morning," he said greeting the attractive visitor with his best public relations smile.

"Good morning," Amanda replied, leaning in to read the gleaming gold name plate pinned to his uniform, "Officer Barnett, I'm here to see Eugene Weems."

"Weems?" Now it made sense, she was probably a

movie star or someone important in the entertainment business, Barnett thought. "You'll be at twelve," he instructed, pointing in the direction of the table they were assigned to. "He'll be out in a minute. If you have any questions, just ask. Have a nice visit," said the congenial officer.

Amanda, following the officer's instruction, walked to the table and had a seat. Officer Barnett's clean cut, brass tacked professional demeanor put her mind at ease. This officer was clearly in control of the visit area and she felt safe.

Looking around, she noticed the other people already visiting at the three dozen tables distributed through the large room. There was one inmate at nearly every short circular table sitting with family and friends. Inmates were clearly recognizable by their blue chambray shirts and dark blue pants with "CDCR prisoner" stenciled in yellow paint. The inmates were squared away with recent haircuts and freshly ironed and creased blues. The visitors appeared dressed in their Sunday best attire and were actively engaged in conversation with their incarcerated loved one. Amanda saw well lighted modern vending machines lined along three of the four walls. The convenient machines contained every sort of food, from candy and ice cream to prepackaged meals. A few of the machines contained soda, juice, water and energy drinks. The food and drinks these machines offered were brand name items, pricy, but the kind of stuff inmates didn't normally have access to. Inmates and their family members were queued at every machine. When an inmate could get a visit, it was a real treat, both emotional and practical.

A young visitor drew Amanda's attention. A five-year-old girl was spreading the contents of a ketchup packet evenly across the CDCR stencil on her father's pants. He was in an intense discussion with the girl's grandfather and hadn't noticed. But her mother did, and when she attempted to stop the young clothing designer, the little girl broke out in tears. She, in her innocence, hoped that by blotting out the stencil, the corrections officers might not notice that he was an inmate and allow her father to come home. Prison was hard on inmates, but sometimes it was harder on the inmate's family, especially the young.

Eugene had been caught off guard when an inmate porter came to his cell door to announce that he had a visit. The porter slid him the handwritten visiting pass through the crack of the cell door and quickly stormed off. Eugene wasn't expecting a visit today from anyone, so his best guess was that it might be Amanda. *She think she slick*, Eugene thought, and smiled to himself. It was a good thing that he believed in the motto of, "Stay ready so you don't have to get ready." He stayed well groomed and kept a set of brand new blues pressed and ready for visiting. He quickly slipped in and out of the shower, brushed his teeth, lotioned up, dressed and headed out of the block to his destination.

When he stepped into the visiting room, he took a moment to scan the scenery for a familiar face, and there it was, gorgeous as a morning sunrise. It was who he hoped it would be, it was Amanda. He admired the angelic being from afar for a brief moment, wanting to mentally savor the view before he approached the table.

The bittersweet scene of a child missing her father was interrupted by a hearty, "Hey, hey, gorgeous." Eugene had arrived, smiling as big as day. Amanda's spirit soared, her heart skipped a beat as she rose to accept Eugene's hug. Dressed in brand new blues, freshly ironed, creased and dialed in to the tee, Eugene took Amanda into his strong muscular arms. Months of love letters culminated in a warm and wonderful embrace. He whispered into her ear, "Damn baby, you hella fine. I think I'ma have to make you my wife."

Pulling back, he grazed her cheek and gave her a gentle kiss.

A surge of excitement shot through her body. He released his hug and took hold of her hands, raising them to his lips. He kissed them gently and Amanda was lost for words. She wanted to speak but was too deep in her fantasy. She couldn't believe she was standing face to face with such a handsome man, who admired everything about her and wanted to be her divine king and life partner. Her eyes spoke the words that her mouth couldn't seem to. Eugene gathered the nerve to do the inevitable; he kissed her painted lips and was surprised by her reaction. They stood there allowing their tongues ample time to get acquainted.

When they parted tongues, Amanda attempted to wipe away the red lipstick from Eugene's lips, but he refused, wanting the proof of the intimate kiss to remain visible. He took hold of her right hand and led her to the podium where he had to check in. He knew the rules, so there was no need for the officer to reiterate them, so he didn't.

Eugene noticed inmates swivel necking to get a glimpse of Amanda's beauty. He also noticed several inmate girlfriends slap the taste out of their mouths for looking at another woman. Eugene didn't feel offended by the gawkers. He purposely walked around the visiting room showcasing his rare gem of a woman, knowing that he would be the talk of the prison. They stopped at the vending machines and Amanda purchased food and drinks for lunch.

As they were returning to their assigned table, Eugene admired her rhythmic hips. They took up a seat next to each other, had lunch, talked, shared laughs and stole kisses. The clandestine smooching was clearly breaking the visiting rules. In the prison visit room there was only one kiss and hug allowed at the beginning of the visit and at the end of the visit, so they had to be careful, love was against the law.

Eugene didn't honestly care about breaking the rule. He hadn't been with a woman in over fourteen years and he had planned on getting as many kisses as he could when the opportunity presented itself. As for Amanda, she did care about the rules and she was a law abiding citizen. The only thing that she did that even came close to breaking a law was when she forgot to pay a parking ticket on time, but she did finally pay the ticket.

They were enjoying each other's company so much; the maximum six hours allowed had quickly flown by. Visiting hours had come to an end. Before Amanda parted, Eugene noticed her happiness disappear. "What's up, babe? You don't seem like yourself," he asked.

"It's nothing, really it's not. I'll tell you tomorrow," she assured him, forcing herself to smile. Eugene pulled her close and laid a parting kiss on her. He knew whatever was on her mind, the kiss would give her something to think about. He couldn't wait for tomorrow.

Amanda returned the next day looking even more beautiful than ever. Heads turned in their direction as usual. The happy couple took pictures to have something to remember the moment. They savored every second together as if it was their last. Time had quickly passed and the visit was coming to an end. Amanda didn't like the feeling of having to leave Eugene. She sincerely wished that she could smuggle him out of the prison. She knew that was impossible and even outrageous wishful thinking, but it was a legitimate desire. Taking hold of Eugene's hands, she leaned in close. He studied her face before looking into her gorgeous hazels. She cleared her throat. It was obvious that she was searching her mind for the right words to communicate whatever it was she needed to say.

"Well Eugene, I had a wonderful time. You are a

gentleman in every sense of the word. I thank you for that. Thank you for making me feel special, loved, and desired again. It's been a while since I had a man give me as much attention as you have. You are really something special. Since we started writing, my feelings for you have flourished and I don't know how to contain them." Amanda took a deep breath before continuing. "What I'm trying to say is that you are a wonderful man, and you deserve someone who you can build a happy life with."

Eugene attempted to speak, but she held up a hand to stop him. "Please, let me finish dear. I have something that I need to tell you." Worry was now plastered over her face. Not knowing how he would take the news she was about to reveal to him, she plunged on. "Eugene, I have recently learned that I have a disease. I have Leukemia, Eugene. Blood cancer. The doctor said I have a chance, but I need a donor, a bone marrow donor. That may be hard to find. And even if there was a donor, I'll still have to go through chemotherapy," Amanda blurted out.

What the... Eugene thought as he stood and pulled her into his arms and held her as close to his heart as he could. He kissed the top of her head and then the bridge of her nose. He lingered for a moment, processing the disturbing news. He silently prayed to the Creator for His help to cure Amanda. He had absolute faith in God because he had witnessed the power of prayer on many occasions, and now he needed God to come through for him one more time.

"Baby, as sure as I stand before you, and I breathe life, I promise you, I will stand by your side through this. We are going to get through this together. We...as in us. The two of us. You hear me? I love you and I'm not about to abandon you."

Amanda was shocked when she heard him say those three powerful words, I love you. She hadn't seen that coming. "Thank you, Eugene. They say my sister can donate bone marrow, so I have a chance. They say with medication and her help, I should be fit as a fiddle in a little while. I just have to get through this." Tears welled up in her eyes at the thought of what the doctors and nurses really said. The truth of the matter was, Amanda had a difficult road ahead of her, and she was frightened.

"I need you," she blurted through her tears. "Why do you got to be locked up here?" She lightly beats on his chest, quietly protesting his imprisonment. "I wish you could just come home with me. I need you," she repeated.

"I know, baby. I'll be out soon. Time will pass, and then we can be together," Eugene promised, wishing he could somehow speed up his sentence. He wiped the tears from her face with his fingertips, then kissed her lips as passionately as he knew how. "My heart belongs to you, babe. I will be your donor. They can take as much bone marrow as they need if it will make you better. If I'm not a match, then I will find you a match. There are thousands of inmates here. I know one of them has to be a match. I can easily pay them a few bucks to donate some of their bone marrow. You know, then that will make you a criminal," he joked, hoping that his humor would bring a smile to Amanda's face. It did, and she loved that about him. She knew he was dead serious about being a donor and for paying an inmate to do so if it came down to that. She wondered if that option was even possible. She gave Eugene one last hug and kiss before she was instructed by a visiting center correctional officer that it was time for her to leave the prison.

Colton noticed something unusual about Eugene when he returned from his Sunday visit. He appeared to be frustrated and depressed. It was unlike him to be moping around and not boasting about his new girlfriend. The question was, what had happened in that timeframe? Colton was concerned and wasn't about to stay quiet about it. Colton gathered his nerves and asked, "Gene, how'd your visit go?"

Eugene looked over toward where Colton was sitting and took up a seat across from him on his own bunk. He put his hands over his face as if he was putting on a hockey mask. He shook his head in a manner of disbelief before raising his head to face his friend.

"I can't believe this shit, man." Tears flooded his eyes. He tried to hold them back, but he couldn't, the flood gates had been ripped open. Colton was shocked and felt a little embarrassed; he had never seen Eugene cry before. It was an emotion that he never suspected Eugene to possess. He had always portrayed a tough guy persona to his roommates and now he was showing an unfamiliar side of himself.

"Can't believe what, doggy?" Colton's concern had begun to turn into distress. Eugene explained, and as he did, it seemed to be draining the life out of him.

"Leukemia? Damn, dogg, that sucks, man. I'm really sorry to hear that," Colton said, commiserating. "You know my sister had leukemia? A few years back my mom visited and gave me the news. It broke my heart. Hearing that my sister was suffering from a horrible disease and I couldn't do anything to help her. I couldn't be there, hug her, nothing. It was a slap in the face and a real wakeup call for me."

"I feel you, man. I remember you mentioning something about that," Eugene recalled.

"I think she is okay now, but when I found out about it...those were hard days. I mean real hard days. Here in the pen there was nothing you can do. I felt like a loser not being able to be there for my little sister when she needed me most, know what I mean?" Colton was feeling the pain of those days all over again now.

"Yeah, man, I sure do," Eugene said solemnly, then asked, "Why don't your family write you?" He had noticed Colton's family didn't write very often.

"My mom writes all the time, but just little updates. There was only so much she can say in a letter. My brother Gregg, we don't see eye to eye. And as for my sisters, Carol and Elizabeth, I haven't the slightest idea. Elizabeth is my little sister, we called her Lizzy. She's the one with leukemia. When we were kids, my dad left. He told me that I would have to step up, "Help your mom out and be the man of the house." I have a lot of memories from back in those days. I was about ten years old and Lizzy was six. I looked out for her, a little overprotective. Someone would knock on our front door and I would go answer. Lizzy would get curious and sneak up behind me to see who it was. If it was a stranger, I would shoo my little sister away, you know what I mean, the way kids are?"

"Yeah." Eugene understood the sweet memory; he had similar memories of his own little cousins.

Colton went on, "Once when we were kids, about that same time, as I recall, my mom wanted to sleep in one Saturday morning. She worked all the time raising the four of us by herself. She was like a superhero or something. But Lizzy and me, we weren't havin' her sleeping in. We wanted poached eggs. We cooked for ourselves all the time, but we liked the way she made those eggs. We needed her to make 'em for us. So I came up with an idea. I had seen union folks picketing on television. The concept made sense to me. If you wanted something, then you got together with other interested parties and deprived the boss of your time until you got what you wanted. Although I wasn't really sure what I was planning to deprive my mom of, with Lizzy by my side I was convinced I had a powerful position. So we made up little picket signs, went into my mom's room while she was asleep, and started marching around like we belonged to the kids union." Smiling, Colton adds

113

sternly, "And let me tell you 'Gene, there better not be any other kids crossing that picket line."

"Did it work?" Eugene inquired.

"Yup," Colton said with a triumphant look. "Poached eggs on toast with ketchup, all we could eat." Waving his hand, he added, "Just like downtown. I've been union ever since. When we were kids, Elizabeth was my best friend. Now that I'm in, she doesn't even write me. She almost died. I haven't seen her in years and I almost lost her forever. But that's how doin' time is. When you're in, everyone forgets about you. It's as if they're trying to punish you even more than the judge did."

"Naw, man, that ain't how it is. They just busy. They living they lives, don't trip. You need to write her and tell how you feel, how you remember those things. You have to let her know how much you miss her and how much you love her. you have to stop being so closed up with your true feelings. The same shit you telling me about how much you miss your little sister, you need to tell her that, write her."

"I did, twenty times," Colton confessed.

"You have to realize, some people don't know how to deal with prison life. Maybe she just don't know what to say. When you got locked up, it's like your family got locked up, too. You don't know how it affected her. You being locked up hurt her; maybe she just don't know how to deal with that. She will come around, but you need to help her by letting her know how much you love her. Trust me, she needs to hear it from you, her big brother, who she looked up to when she was young. You need to handle that before it's too late," Eugene said, offering his advice.

"Maybe," Colton agreed. "Anyway, I guess the doctors fixed her up. They got some dynamite treatments for leukemia nowadays. I guess she got lucky; she was treated at this place in Los Angeles, some kind of high tech cancer center. I'll write my mom and get the address. Maybe Amanda could check it out," Colton suggested.

"Yeah, cool, that would be a big help," Eugene agreed, appreciating Colton's concern. "What ever happened to that girl you were tellin' me about? The one you sent that portrait of Marilyn Monroe to?" Eugene asked, trying to change the subject because he noticed Colton was venturing into depression and thinking about the disconnection between he and his family.

"I love that girl, but it's the same thing, I've been down too long. Everybody moves on. she didn't write me back," Colton said despairingly.

"Did you try writing her again?" Eugene asked.

"Wrote her twice. No response," Colton was attempting to end the painful conversation.

"Well, don't trip. You'll be out someday and you can go see her," Eugene encouraged, but he didn't really believe in seeking out past relationships with people who had turned their backs on a friend in need.

"Yeah, maybe. I sure would like to hear from her now, though, but I guess that's how it is, at least for me anyway. But you got Amanda. That's a good thing. I hope everything works out."

"Me, too," Eugene said thoughtfully, with worry in his voice. He appreciated his friend's patience in acting as a listening board and attempting to help heal him from his emotional wound. However, placing a band-aid on a cut that needed stitches was worthless. Eugene's dreams of a new life were dashed, but he wouldn't give up that easily.

He needed information about leukemia. He had questions and needed answers. He had no intention of allowing Amanda to go down this road alone. Not if he could help it.

Chapter 13

I was successful in achieving my goal. The surprise vacation was much needed and it was the right idea for winning my husband over. It seemed like old times. For me, it felt like I was on our honeymoon again, but even better. It was fresh and new, I was wiser, more experienced and thoughtful.

My confidence was validated by the marvelous new sense of excitement Richard introduced into the bedroom. Our partnership was strengthened, I felt closer to him, but I could not help but wonder what the hell had gotten into him. Never had my husband been so sexual, sensual and attentive. With sentimental aggression he bent, twisted and caressed my body into different sex positions and even spanked my rear-end. I was astonished with my husband's energy and how he brought my body so many pleasures.

I was thankful for whatever it was that triggered the sexual beast within Richard and I hoped that the fire within his loins would continue to roar. I picked up my cell phone and tapped in a message on the touch screen before sitting it back down on the nightstand.

Eugene had returned early from his vocational office services class to find Colton lying on his bunk staring aimlessly at a piece of paper he was holding inches from his face. "What's up, square? Whatcha doin' home so early?" Eugene inquired playfully. Colton ignored the question. He was lost somewhere in a world of his own. Eugene knew it was common for Colton to zone out, closing out the world around him. However, Eugene did not like to be ignored. He felt ornery and was now curious to know what was on the piece of paper that held his friend's attention captive. He walked over and snatched the paper from Colton's hand.

"What's this?" Eugene began reading the contents.

"A one-twenty-eight. A cop over on D-yard wrote me up. He said I was sitting on his bench," Colton attempted to explain. He had not taken offense at having the paper snatched from his hands. He knew that was Eugene's way of getting his attention.

"How the hell a cop going to write you up for sitting on a bench. Ain't no cops own no benches in prison. He lost his mind. That write-up ain't going nowhere. It will be dismissed soon as the lieutenant hears it."

"It's a one-twenty-eight counseling chrono; they don't have hearings on them," Colton stated firmly. He was correct; counseling chronos could not be challenged and correctional officers knew this. They also knew that the chrono remained in the inmate's file indefinitely and could affect a lifer's parole date up to fifteen years, and Colton was a lifer. He was also the secretary on the Inmate Advisory Council. A five-man council that represented the thirty-five hundred inmates at the institution. Council members were under constant pressure. As liaisons between inmates and prison staff, they were expected to sift through various complaints on both sides and assist in advising and providing solutions for the institution. Considering prison politics, it was a challenging position, to say the least.

Eugene was the Parliamentarian on the Council and had helped Colton get elected because he knew Colton was an intelligent team player who had effective communication and interpersonal skills. He knew Colton would remain loyal and uphold the dignity of what the council stood for. The three other members were hustlers, but they all genuinely believed in providing a voice for inmates at department head and warden's meetings.

Although it was high pressure, Colton considered the job a privilege and enjoyed working with people like Daniel "Danny" Lanning, the President of the Council. Danny had the respect of a large network of inmates due to his skillful organization of the largest prison sports leagues and tournaments in the CDCR, second only to the legendary inmate leagues at San Quentin State Prison. In meetings with staff, Danny pushed hard for things that the inmate population wanted.

Then there was Henry "Paya" Ortiz, the Vice-President of the Council, a fast talker with a cholo persona. Paya was notorious for his energy in support of self-help groups. Spending most of his time in the IEC office working on Self-Awareness in Recovery (SAR), a popular self-help group he co-founded. Paya had a large constituency of inmates throughout the prison who believed in positive programming and preparing inmates for release. Paya did everything he could to help out.

Last, but not least, there was Happy. In the CDCR, the Americans with Disabilities Act (ADA) was taken very seriously. Warden Ron Davis was no exception. He created a paid position, a few cents an hour for an inmate ADA representative to sit on the Institutional Council. Esrom "Happy" Madrid was a veteran of the street wars and had a lengthy sentence and a bullet in his spine to prove it. Fortunately, he was not paralyzed and left in a wheelchair; he only needed a cane and his mental state was reasonably intact. His passion, motivation and experience dealing with ADA issues made him the right person for the job.

Valley State Prison inmates were lucky to have these guys speaking up for them. They worked hard to create an institution that benefitted everyone; staff, prisoners and society. The five men were loyal to each other, always in good humor and of the same mind. It was an extraordinary council. However, the one-twenty-eight write-up that Colton received was the straw that broke the camel's back. It had been his second disciplinary write-up since taking the job and it was clearly retaliatory. Colton was always respectful and quiet, especially around the prison staff. He did not speak unless spoken to; he was the nerd of the IEC. But sadly, some correctional officers took offense to inmates having access to the administration and sometimes would retaliate with arbitrary and inaccurate write-ups.

Colton had stayed back in the IEC office a little later than usual. He had been researching leukemia on his computer's Encarta, trying to find something positive he could take back to Eugene. Colton had missed his usual unlock and so decided to exit through the D-side gate to return to his respective yard. Patient as always, he took up a seat in the shade out of the hundred degree California sun. He waited for an officer to key the D-yard gate so he could return to B-yard where he was housed. When an officer showed up, he was not there to open a gate. He was there to lay down the law about why an inmate was sitting on the bench outside the program office. The officer knew Colton worked in the program office and had an IEC privilege card that granted him access to all program offices and yards. It was obvious the officer couldn't care less about any of that.

As the Institutional Secretary, Colton was taking too much heat, he would have to resign.

"Looks like I'm gonna have to quit," Colton stated. "But that's cool. I'll have some free time on my hands. I'll be able to write letters to leukemia organizations to find out what we can do. That's way more important than worrying about prison politics and write-ups."

"Yeah, that's what's up," Eugene agreed solemnly. He did not like the idea of Colton quitting, but saw the wisdom in his decision. In prison. Everybody had their problems, but leukemia was life or death and all Eugene could think about was Amanda.

Amanda received a text message from MaryAnn and cringed. "Hi Amanda, call me," it read. She really didn't feel like arguing with MaryAnn right now. She felt horrible. She had begun chemotherapy and her physical and emotional state was in a nose dive. The world was becoming a gray and sometimes depressing place. Amanda did not have the patience or strength to deal with more negativity. She had not told MaryAnn about her diagnosis. Therefore, in self-defense, she blasted out a text, "I have leukemia. I am in chemo. I don't need your shit right now!" Within seconds, Amanda's phone was ringing. She answered, hoping MaryAnn would be nice to her.

"Amanda!" MaryAnn nearly shouted. "If you're kidding around, that's not something to be joking about, it's not funny. Leukemia is a dreadful disease. It destroys a person's immune system. People who get this disease require a bone marrow transplant, and that's if they're lucky enough to find a matching donor. But even then, it's terrible, and a long shot for recovery. People that really have leukemia go through a lot. They have to go through chemo, radiation, and take anti-rejection drugs for the rest of their lives. It's a nightmare and it's something that you shouldn't be joking about," MaryAnn scolded. The phone went silent for a moment.

"I know," Amanda whimpers into the phone. "That's what they told me." Tears streamed down her cheeks.

"Amanda...my God.. Amanda, really?" Fear clutched at MaryAnn's heart as the cold reality unfolded. "You're serious!" Then, with desperation in her voice, "Oh no, Mandy," she cried, using the nickname from their childhood. Amanda's silence confirmed MaryAnn's concern. Her lifelong friend was in trouble. "I'm catching the first flight home. Do you have a good doctor?"

"Yes, I really lucked out. The people at the hospital are wonderful. Some of the best in the world."

"Okay, good. I'll be there soon. I'll take care of you," MaryAnn offered, thinking how sweet her best friend was and how much she loved her. Memories of their childhood shuffled through her mind. Tears began to flood in MaryAnn's eyes at the thought of possibly losing her best friend. "I'm so sorry about everything, Amanda. I'm sorry about what I said about Eugene and how I treated you. I love you and miss you," MaryAnn apologized, realizing how selfish she had been. Having recently rejuvenated her own happiness, she wanted Amanda to be happy as well, but more than anything, she wanted her best friend to live.

"Yeah, yeah, yeah...apologies are accepted, so don't be getting all mushy on me. But thank you, girl. Eugene and his million letters have been the only bright spot in my life. He is the only thing that makes me happy and keeps me strong."

"I know, sweetheart. I'll see you soon, okay? And tell Eugene that I said hi."

"Okay, will do. See you soon," Amanda whispered. Both women cried tears of joy and sadness together over the phone for a moment before ending the call.

Chapter 14

Amanda's doctors had set up seemingly endless appointments for her treatment. Treating leukemia required using harsh chemicals to kill the cancer, but in so doing, the chemicals destroy the patient's immune system. Fortunately, Amanda's sister Jessica had the same blood type and was a prime donor because she also had the constitution of a horse, proven by her four healthy children. Amanda had reason to be hopeful, but she was not enjoying her body being flushed with toxic chemicals and having to live in isolation. Chemo made her weak and subjected her to further illnesses, even a common cold could kill. Hospital staff went to great lengths to protect her from infectious viruses and bacteria. She was instructed to avoid all public places, especially a public institution like a prison. She would not be able to visit Eugene. Depression had set in. It had become a task just to drag herself out of bed.

There was a sharp thump on her front door. The thunderous sound shattered the still silence that had crystallized in her home. Reluctantly, Amanda rose out of bed to answer the door.

"Amanda, are you there? It's me." The familiar voice echoed from the outside. It couldn't be MaryAnn, she thought, reaching to unlock the deadbolt. How could it be? She was in South American with her husband. She must have...a smile broke across her face as she opened the door. It was evident that MaryAnn cared deeply about her.

When MaryAnn said she would get on the first flight home, evidently, she meant chartering a private jet immediately. Sometimes being a multimillionaire had real advantages.

Amanda watched her wealthy, powerful and loyal friends walk through the foyer. Both Richard and MaryAnn had looks of concern on their faces, but all Amanda could think of was how did they get here so quickly? A warm, secure feeling of support overwhelmed her and she began to cry.

"Mandy, are you okay?" MaryAnn asked.

"Yes, I'm fine...now." Although it was against doctor's orders, it was hugs all around.

After learning about leukemia, blood cancers and their various treatments, Eugene had a better understanding of Amanda's plight. Although he couldn't physically be there to support her, he most definitely made his presence felt through his many letters and phone calls. He poured his heart, soul and love into every written letter he sent her. His written words kept her happy and looking forward to the future beyond her disease.

In him, she had found a special, exotic, and true love. She had found the Green Rose.

THE END

ABOUT THE AUTHORS

Eugene L. Weems is the bestselling author of *United We Stand, Prison Secrets, America's Most Notorious Gangs, The Other Side of the Mirror, Head Gamez, Bound by Loyalty, Red Beans and Dirty Rice for the Soul, Innocent by Circumstance, Cold as Ice, and The Green Rose.* The former kick boxing champion is a producer, model, philanthropist, and founder of No Question Apparel, Inked Out Beef Books, and co-founder of Vibrant Green for Vibrant Peace. He is from Las Vegas, Nevada.

Clarke Lowe is co-author of *America's Most Notorious Gangs, Red Beans and Dirty Rice for the Soul,* and co-founder of Vibrant Green for Vibrant Peace. He is a commercial diver, journeyman structural ironworker, drug and alcohol counselor and holds a bachelor's of science degree in psychology. He is currently serving a life sentence in the California state prison system.

BOUND BY LOYALTY

COREY 'C-MURDER' MILLER
EUGENE L. WEEMS

The novel that critics across the nation are raving about and people are eager to read.

C-Murder and Weems constructed an elaborate contemporary urban thriller full of twists and false starts. Bound by Loyalty is absolutely chilling and bursting with surprises.

$14.95   278pgs   6x9 Paperback   ISBN: 978-0991238002
Celebrity Spotlight Entertainment, LLC

RED BEANS and DIRTY RICE FOR THE SOUL

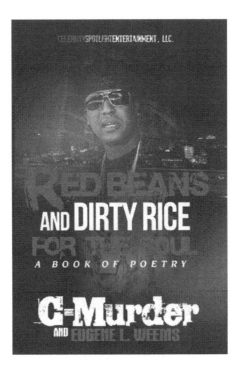

COREY 'C-MURDER' MILLER
EUGENE L. WEEMS
CLARKE LOWE

Tread the gutta' life with **C-MURDER** in this gripping compilation of poetry that is deeply rooted in the streets and behind prison walls.

WARNING! May cause a severe reaction or death in people who are square to the game. If an allergic reaction occurs, stop reading and seek emergency counseling from your local priest.

$14.95   103pgs   6x9 Paperback   ISBN: 978-0991238019
Celebrity Spotlight Entertainment, LLC

UNITED WE STAND

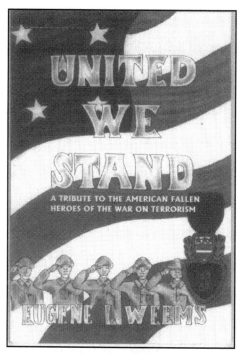

A TRIBUTE TO THE AMERICAN FALLEN
HEROES OF THE WAR ON TERRORISM
Eugene L. Weems

United We Stand is a beautiful collection of inspirational artwork and passion-filled poetry created as a living tribute to the American troops who have made the ultimate sacrifice for our country in the war against terrorism.

100% of the proceeds from this book will be contributed to provide care packages for the active duty troops who remain engaged in the war overseas and provide college scholarship trust funds for the children of our American fallen heroes.

$14.95   95 pgs   6x9 Paperback   ISBN: 978-1-4251-9130-6
Celebrity Spotlight Entertainment, LLC

3 STRIKES

CRUCIFIX

Growing up poor, abused and surrounded by violence, Tito Lopez dreamed of becoming a cop. But as fate would have it, his dreams became a series of nightmares and the treachery of life in the hood overtakes him.

When the water gets too deep, gangsters pull Tito out, embrace him and become his family. Unfortunately, Tito is drawn into a life of crime and gangsterism, which involves the Mexican Mafia and corrupt cops.

This gripping reality takes you on a journey leading to betrayal and a Three Strikes life sentence.

$14.95   187 pgs   6x9 Paperback   ISBN: 978-0-9912380-3-3
Celebrity Spotlight Entertainment, LLC

PRISON SECRETS
2nd EDITION

EUGENE L. WEEMS

Once recognized as a ruthless killer and remorseless criminal, Lyle Menendez remains housed in a maximum security correctional facility with other notorious murderers and gang members. In this level 4 maximum security prison, even one of America's most notorious murderers could be victimized. This novel will unlock the doors to all the prison secrets; weapons manufacturing, drug smuggling, prison rapes, gang politics, officer corruption and much, much more.

$14.95   183 pgs   6x9 Paperback   ISBN: 978-1500934873
Celebrity Spotlight Entertainment, LLC

COLD AS ICE

**A.C. BELLARD
EUGENE L. WEEMS**

Cold As Ice, an urban thriller that reads like a Hollywood movie script. This cutting edge murder mystery has twists, turns, and suspense that will keep a reader's mind intrigued to the very end.

Which character will you root for?

$14.95   212 pgs   6x9 Paperback   ISBN: 978-1500959562
Celebrity Spotlight Entertainment, LLC

INNOCENT BY CIRCUMSTANCE

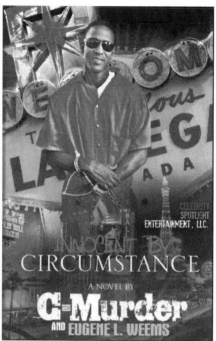

C-MURDER
EUGENE L. WEEMS

The day of his grandmother's death was the day Boo began his quest for survival in the fast-paced, treacherous and wicked streets of Las Vegas, Nevada. The grieving child is forced into hustling, larceny, burglary, robbery and even murder just to maintain the necessities of life. Boo, Jewel and the rest of the kids exact revenge for the brutal crimes committed against them. They find unconditional love, commitment and loyalty within each other and become a family unit.

This action-filled story will surprise the reader with sensitive and all too real situations. A compelling novel with deep, complex characters guilty of horrible crimes...or are they Innocent by Circumstance?

$14.95   202 pgs   6x9 Paperback   ISBN: 978-1503355798
Celebrity Spotlight Entertainment, LLC

Made in the USA
Middletown, DE
04 February 2018